PLAY BY PLAY

A SWEETGUM MEADOWS ROMANCE BOOK 11

IMANI PRICE

First Edition: October 2025

ISBN 978-1-960207-66-1 (ebook)
ISBN 978-1-960207-67-8 (paperback)

Published by Books to Hook Publishing, LLC.
www.BooksToHook.com

CONTENTS

PROLOGUE

Sweetgum Meadows High School, Graduation Night

Hakeem Brown stood at the edge of the football field, the hum of distant cicadas and the crackle of the stadium lights playing a tender symphony in the summer air. The bleachers above him were nearly empty now that the ceremony was over. A few stray programs fluttered across the ground like restless birds, reminders of all the pomp and celebration that had ended just an hour earlier.

He swallowed hard. His heart felt heavier than any defensive tackle he'd ever faced. All season, all year, he'd relished the promise of freedom beyond Sweetgum—the thrill of a college scholarship, the dream of someday playing pro ball. But tonight, that dream felt too big and too complicated to share with the girl he loved.

Jada Davis was waiting for him on the lowest step of the bleachers, legs tucked beneath her. She wore her maroon graduation robe half-zipped, her mortarboard abandoned on the bench beside her. Dark curls spilled down her shoulders. When she saw him approach, her entire face lit up with a smile so bright it made his chest ache.

"There you are," she teased, patting the wooden seat beside her. "I thought my star quarterback might've gotten lost in the crowd of adoring fans."

Despite his inner turmoil, Hakeem smiled. "Nah, I'm right here." He eased down next to her, their shoulders touching. For a moment, they simply breathed in the night—two kids on the brink of adulthood.

"I was thinking..." Jada's voice was soft, hopeful. "In the fall, you'll be at State on your full ride, and I'll be at Southeastern for my undergrad in kinesiology. It's two hours apart, but we'll make it work, right?"

Her eyes shone with such unwavering faith that Hakeem had to force himself not to look away. Instead, he reached for her hand. It felt impossibly small in his. The weight of the decision he'd made pressed down on him like a thousand-pound barbell.

"Jada..." His voice came out raw. "I've been thinking about this a lot."

She glanced up, the smile faltering just a fraction. "Okay...?"

He ran his thumb over her knuckles. So many memories lived in that single touch: the way they'd clung to each other after every win, every loss, every late-night study session. She was home in a way few things had ever been. But that was exactly why he had to let her go.

"You're gonna be incredible," he said, forcing gentleness into each syllable. "You'll be focused on your program, and I'll be at college training, playing ball, trying to stand out enough to get noticed by scouts. We'll both be chasing big dreams."

Her gaze searched his. "We can chase them together."

His stomach twisted. "I thought so, too. But...long-distance is hard, Jada. We'll both be so busy. I don't—I don't want us to get resentful. I don't want the pressure of our relationship to hold you back from...from everything you could be."

Her hand stiffened in his. "Hold me back? Hakeem, you're the best thing that's ever happened to me. You've never held me back."

He couldn't bear to see the first shimmer of tears in her eyes, but he made himself face it. "I don't want to lose you," he whispered, voice cracking. "But if we try to keep this going and it falls apart later—" He shook his head. "It'll hurt more. Maybe—maybe we should make a clean break now, so we can both give our futures one hundred percent."

Jada blinked, her lips parted in disbelief. "You...want to break up?"

He could practically feel her heart pounding in her chest the same way his own hammered in his. Everything in him screamed to pull her close and take it all back. Instead, he forced himself to nod, the word cutting him deeper than any injury on the field ever had. "Yes."

She let out a shaky breath. Tears gathered along her lashes but didn't fall. "Why? Why can't we just try?"

Hakeem's vision blurred. He inhaled, fighting for composure. "Because I can't stand the thought of seeing you hurt if this doesn't work out. And I can't fail at football before I even begin. I—this is my only shot, Jada."

Silence fell, thick and suffocating. Finally, she withdrew her hand. His palm felt cold without her warmth.

"You think letting me go won't hurt me?" She rose to her feet, voice trembling. Her eyes shone with devastation. "Hakeem, I love you...did you even think about that?"

"Every second," he answered, standing as well. Desperation tugged at his chest. "But I truly believe this is best for both of us."

For one breathless moment, Jada didn't move. Then she reached for her mortarboard, hugging it against her, and turned away. He watched the slender lines of her shoulders begin to shake.

Hakeem forced his feet to remain planted. He wanted nothing more than to pull her into his arms, promise her that none of this mattered, that they would conquer every distance in the world. But he didn't. He let her walk away under the lights of the empty stadium, her quiet sobs tearing at his heart.

Long after she disappeared from sight, he stood alone beneath the hush of the Georgia night, grappling with the certainty he'd just broken the heart of the only girl he'd ever loved. And in doing so, he might've broken his own.

CHAPTER ONE

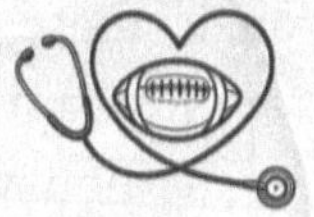

Present Day

Hakeem Brown slumped against the exam table of the Atlanta Orthopedic & Sports Medicine Clinic, the crisp white paper crackling beneath his weight. He tried to focus on the orthopedic specialist's words, but the details washed over him in a steady drone. Partial ACL tear. Severe cartilage damage. A longer recovery timeline than anticipated. Each bleak phrase knotted his stomach tighter.

Dr. Hayes, a man with kind eyes and salt-and-pepper hair, placed Hakeem's medical chart aside. "You've got a tough road ahead," he said gently. "Even with top-notch therapy, returning to NFL standards is…unlikely."

Unlikely. The word rattled Hakeem's chest like a fresh impact. He'd heard rumors of this outcome in hushed locker-room corners, from his agent, from the wary looks of team trainers. But hearing it stated so plainly hammered the reality home.

"How long?" he managed, voice rough. If any shred of hope remained, he needed a concrete timeline.

"Nine months to a year, at least," Dr. Hayes explained. "Lots of therapy and patience. Ideally, you should be somewhere quieter than Atlanta—fewer distractions, more time to recover. Go home, focus on rehab."

Home. The suggestion landed like a quiet echo, conjuring images of farmland, rolling meadows, and the sweet, earthy air of his family's dairy farm. For a split second, he almost heard a girl's laugh drifting through those fields—a memory he'd carried no matter how far he'd traveled. But he forced the thought aside. The bigger question was what now: his NFL future teetered on a knife's edge.

He stood on unsteady legs, offering Dr. Hayes a firm handshake. "Thank you, sir," he said, voice tight with an undercurrent of dread. "I appreciate everything."

With a resigned nod, the doctor stepped out. Left alone, Hakeem struggled against the urge to punch the exam table—anger licking at him for the abrupt end to what he'd worked his entire life for. But an athlete's body didn't last forever. He'd always known that. He just thought he'd have more time.

Less than an hour later, he navigated congested city streets, heading back to his high-rise. Storm clouds brooded overhead, matching the turmoil in his thoughts. Inside the sleek lobby, he ignored the doorman's polite nod, riding the elevator up in tense silence.

His apartment felt hollow when he stepped in—cool modern decor, floor-to-ceiling windows, all once a point of pride. Now it seemed like a box storing the remnants of a life that might never be the same. He tossed his keys on the quartz countertop, the dull echo revealing the emptiness he was used to. In the NFL, relationships rarely ran deep—some casual dating here and there, but nothing lasting. *Not since her,* he admitted to himself, heart twinging.

He dropped onto the leather couch, staring out at the cityscape. Atlanta's vibrant energy had always thrilled him—until now. Now it felt suffocating. *The doctor said go somewhere quieter.* But was it worth slinking back to Sweetgum Meadows, the place he couldn't wait to leave at eighteen? The place that still conjured a thousand old memories, most of them colored by a girl's laughter and a heartbreak he never truly shook?

He rubbed his stiff knee, wincing at the dull throb. Therapy in a calmer environment might do him good. After all, the city reminded him of constant workouts and the relentless press of NFL expectations he might never fulfill again.

In the hush, his phone buzzed once—just an agent update he had no energy to read. He glanced at the device, throat tight. *Her phone number was still in there, right? Did she change it?* He'd never had the courage to find out.

With a sigh, he set the phone aside. That was a door he wasn't sure he could open, not now. But he couldn't stay here either, surrounded by the ghost of a career that might be gone. He needed time, space to heal—physically, definitely, and maybe emotionally too. And for that, there was only one real place to go.

Rising, he limped to the bedroom. The reflection in the mirror startled him: exhausted eyes, shoulders sagging under the weight of lost dreams. Outside, thunder rumbled, lightning flashing across the skyline. *When did life get this bleak?* He remembered a simpler time—back in Sweetgum, wide-eyed with hope.

He pushed the thought aside, flicking off the bedroom light. By daybreak, he'd be on the road to that small town he once dismissed. He had no idea if that meant reuniting with the life he left behind. *I'm only going there to rehab my knee, away from this constant reminder of what I've lost,* he told himself.

And yet, as he shoved clothes into a duffel, the image of her —laughing in a summer field—lingered at the edges of his mind, stubborn and unwavering, the one thing Atlanta's bright lights had never erased.

CHAPTER TWO

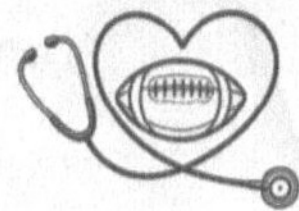

*J*ada Davis climbed the narrow staircase to her new studio apartment off of Main Street in Sweetgum Meadows. A single box pressed firmly against her hip. The aged steps creaked in greeting, the sound echoing through the quiet hallway. Outside the windows, dusk had begun its slow descent. Painting Main Street in soft shades of gold. For a split second, she let herself linger—eyes closed, heart stumbling over memories of a time when life felt simpler.

Of course, *he* surfaced in those memories like a stubborn echo: Hakeem Brown, star quarterback and her first true love. She had no business dwelling on him. Not after all these years. Not after the way he'd crushed her so completely.

She exhaled, pushing that thought away with a measured breath. *I'm only here for my career,* she reminded herself. *A temporary contract at Sweetgum Hospital, then on to bigger opportunities in sports therapy.* She would not let old heartbreak steal her focus.

Inside her studio, she set down the box and switched on the lone lamp by the door. The cozy space smelled faintly of fresh paint and her half-opened cardboard boxes. She couldn't pretend the nostalgia wasn't there. Sweetgum was the place she and Hakeem had once woven an entire future in their heads—a future that never happened.

Her phone buzzed. She pulled it from her pocket, glancing at the screen. It was a text from her mom:

> If you need help unpacking, we're just a few blocks away. Don't be shy!

Jada couldn't help but smile. She typed a quick reply—

> I'm good for now, love you!

—then placed the phone aside. Leaning against the kitchenette counter, she surveyed her apartment. Her stomach rumbled at the reminder that she hadn't eaten since breakfast. The fridge was empty, and her cooking supplies were still buried somewhere in a sealed box.

Guess that means takeout, she thought, letting her hunger guide her to the one place she knew would be open this late on Main Street—*the diner.* Only, it wasn't *Rochelle's* diner anymore. Rochelle Stevens had retired months ago. Now, her nephew Malachi ran the place with his fiancée, Aimee—a fact Jada had pieced together from local chatter and the occasional social media update. It still felt odd to imagine the diner without Rochelle in her usual corner booth, swirling coffee and dispensing gossip. But from what Jada heard, Aimee and Malachi had kept the menu's best staples alive while adding a few fresh twists.

She grabbed her purse and headed out. The evening air clung gently to her skin, carrying the faint smell of magnolias. As she strolled along Main Street, she couldn't help noticing how it felt both familiar and changed: the local bookstore's window boasted a newer sign, the Chinese restaurant had updated its decor, and there were more out-of-town visitors than she remembered. Growth. Progress. And yet, the same lamp posts and quaint brick facades stood unchanged.

Arriving at the diner, she hesitated under the vintage marquee that now read: *Rochelle's Old-Fashioned Diner – Under New Ownership.* A wave of nostalgia tightened her chest. She could still see her eighteen-year-old self standing in almost the same spot, waiting for Hakeem to wrap an arm around her shoulders as they walked in together. Shaking the memory free, she pushed open the door. The overhead bell jingled, welcoming her inside.

Warm light, the smell of fried chicken, and the low hum of conversation washed over her. The familiar black-and-white checkered floor remained, but she noticed the walls had fresh paint and new photos—some of the staff, some of local events. A small chalkboard sign near the counter advertised *Aimee's Seasonal Specials!* in cheerful script.

From behind the hostess stand appeared a tall man with a broad smile—Malachi, if Jada remembered correctly. He inclined his head in greeting. "Welcome to Rochelle's Old-Fashioned Diner. Need a table for one?"

"Yes, please." She offered a small smile. "If it's no trouble."

His eyes crinkled warmly. "No trouble at all. Anywhere you like. You want a menu or are you here for Aimee's specials?"

Jada's brow arched curiously. "Let's see the specials. I'm feeling adventurous tonight."

Malachi chuckled, handing over a laminated sheet with whimsical doodles. "Coming right up. Aimee will be thrilled."

He stepped aside to seat another customer while Jada slipped into a booth along the window. The gentle murmurs of other patrons filled the space with a cozy, neighborly vibe. Over by the pass-through window, a woman with a bright smile—Aimee, presumably—coordinated orders with a couple of line cooks. She radiated friendly confidence, so different from the retired Rochelle's style, yet the diner still felt...comforting.

Jada skimmed the specials menu: "Pumpkin Bisque," "Honey-Glazed Chicken with a Sweetgum Twist," and an "Autumn Apple Crisp" for dessert. Her stomach grumbled in approval.

Moments later, Aimee herself approached. Her curly hair was pulled back into a tidy ponytail, and a streak of flour dusted her left hip—probably from a quick stint in the kitchen. "Hey there, I'm Aimee." She flashed an easy grin. "See anything you like?"

Jada nodded, returning the smile. "The bisque sounds perfect. And maybe a side of cornbread if you have it?"

"Cornbread, absolutely," Aimee replied, scribbling on her notepad. "Coming right up. Welcome back to Sweetgum, by the way." She tapped the notepad lightly. "Word travels fast around here."

Heat burned in Jada's cheeks. *Small towns. Some things never change.* "Thanks, I...haven't been here for years. Still getting used to it."

Aimee's smile was empathetic. "I understand. I grew up in a different part of Georgia and moved here a couple years ago. Sweetgum definitely has its charms once you settle in." She paused, then gestured at Jada. "Hey, if you need anything, holler. We're glad to have you."

Once Aimee headed back toward the kitchen, Jada took a breath. The easy warmth of the exchange felt reassuring...until her gaze flicked to an old photograph hanging near the diner's entrance. It showed the Sweetgum High football team celebrating a victory—Hakeem front and center, helmet hoisted in triumph. Even from across the room, her heart lurched at the memory of that night. She blinked, tearing her eyes away.

He's probably still playing for the NFL, she told herself. The last she heard, he was a rising star. The thought both panged her heart and sparked a strange flash of pride. She hated that she still cared about his success.

Her phone buzzed against the tabletop, pulling her from the swirl of memories. She glanced down to see a message from her childhood friend, Aliyah:

> Girl, I heard you're back! We need to catch up.
> Let's grab coffee tomorrow?

The corners of Jada's lips lifted. *Aliyah.* The very mention of her friend brought a sense of home. She typed a quick reply—

> Sounds great! Let's do it

—and set the phone aside just as Aimee returned with a steaming bowl of pumpkin bisque. The scent of cinnamon and nutmeg filled the booth.

"Careful, it's hot," Aimee said, placing a small basket of fresh cornbread next to it. "Enjoy."

"Thanks," Jada murmured, inhaling deeply. "Smells amazing."

As soon as Aimee left, Jada dipped her spoon into the bisque. The first taste was velvety and rich, a subtle sweetness layered with warm spices. A tiny moan of delight escaped her—she hadn't realized how hungry she was. Or maybe the comfort of sweet, hearty soup reminded her of simpler times.

But her peace was short-lived. Every bite seemed to remind her that *he* wasn't here to share it. She could almost hear his playful voice: *Is that my cornbread you're stealing, Jada?* Or the way he'd flash that crooked grin anytime she tried to feed him a spoonful of soup. She squeezed her eyes shut, willing the memories to vanish.

When she opened them, the diner remained—the same checkered floors, the same hum of conversation. But Rochelle wasn't buzzing around with a coffeepot and a friendly quip. Hakeem wasn't waiting for her in the next booth. Everything was different, yet the reminders were everywhere.

She forced her attention back to the bisque, pushing the

painful thoughts aside. *Focus on the future.* She was here to build her career, polish her skills in physical therapy, and then move on to a bigger city, a bigger stage. She had to keep that in mind whenever her heart threatened to steer her back into the past.

A slight pang tugged in her chest—an ache she had never quite managed to soothe. *You weren't enough to keep him,* a small voice whispered. She'd spent years convincing herself it was a mercy they ended things before college. But the truth was, she'd spent just as long mourning him, mourning what could have been.

With a shaky breath, she finished the bisque. Around her, the diner's energy wound down, a few customers settling tabs. She observed Malachi moving about, chatting with patrons, occasionally catching Aimee's eye to exchange some private joke. They had the easy warmth of two people in love. That realization stung, and she hated herself for the flicker of envy it ignited.

She paid her bill at the cash register, where Aimee reappeared with a friendly wave. "Hope you liked the soup. It's one of my seasonal favorites."

"It was fantastic," Jada assured her. "Thanks...really."

Aimee beamed. "Come by anytime. We're always trying new recipes, and we'd love to have your feedback."

With a polite nod, Jada stepped back out onto Main Street. Twilight had deepened, the moon perched low over the rooftops. As she walked, the diner's neon glow faded behind her, replaced by the silent companionship of closed shops and parked cars.

The hush of night pressed in. She clutched her purse a little tighter, feeling an old wound throb in her chest. Being back in Sweetgum was going to test her in ways she hadn't fully prepared for. But she would endure it, just as she'd endured everything else.

She glanced toward the edge of town, where rolling farmland lay under a blanket of early-evening stars. *He's probably miles away,* she thought, *living his dream.* It was a dream he'd once claimed she couldn't be part of. She shook off the sting and quickened her pace, determined to keep moving forward.

It didn't matter if old wounds ached. She was a different person now, stronger than the naive teenager who'd crumpled under heartbreak. She'd found a purpose all her own: healing others through physical therapy, dedicating herself to sports medicine. *That* was her mission—*not* dredging up the past with someone who'd cast her aside.

Yet as she climbed the stairs to her apartment and turned the key in the lock, a single thought slipped through her defenses:

Why does it still hurt so much?

She had no answer. Only the echo of her footsteps against the worn floorboards and the quiet awareness that returning to Sweetgum meant facing every piece of her broken heart—no matter how hard she tried to hide it.

CHAPTER THREE

*H*akeem pulled his pickup truck to a stop along the curb and stared out at the familiar sign: Rochelle's Old-Fashioned Diner.

He killed the engine and sat there, wrestling with the knot in his stomach. Once upon a time, he couldn't wait to blow out of Sweetgum Meadows, get a taste of the wider world. But now, as he watched a pair of old friends amble out of the diner's front door, exchanging boisterous goodbyes, the irony bit at him. He was the one returning, older and bruised, unsure of how to fit back into the place he once called home.

You're doing this, he told himself. His left knee twinged in response, as though echoing the uncertainty he felt. He was supposed to be all about second chances—second chance at a life beyond football, second chance at love if he could be so lucky. But the memory of Jada's face lingered in his mind: the tears in her eyes that night, the disbelief threaded through the heartbreak when he said goodbye. He still felt the scorch of that moment, even years later.

He inhaled and pushed out of the truck. The late-summer sun pressed against his shoulders. Familiar porch bells jingled overhead as he stepped inside. The transition from bright daylight to the diner's cozy glow brought a wash of nostalgia. Everything smelled of fried chicken, yeast rolls, and the faint tang of fresh coffee. He hadn't realized how much he'd missed that scent—so *homey* it nearly made his knees buckle more than the old injury.

"Oh my goodness! Hakeem Brown," a warm voice exclaimed.

He glanced over to see an older woman sitting at the counter —Mrs. Andrews, one of the members of the "hit-and-run" squad of fit, older women who frequently power-walked the streets of Sweetgum if memory served—her eyes shining with recognition. Others turned at the name, and whispers darted around the room: *Did you hear? Hakeem's back.*

Heat crawled up his neck. He hadn't exactly announced his return, hoping he could ease into town quietly. Clearly, that plan was out the window. *Small towns,* he reminded himself. *They never change.*

"Haven't seen you since Rashad's wedding," Mrs. Andrews continued, coming over to him to pat him on the shoulder as if welcoming a prodigal son. "Heard about your injury. So sorry, dear."

"Thanks," Hakeem murmured, mustering a polite smile. "I'm, uh, just here to grab a bite."

Mrs. Andrews ushered him toward a booth near the window, but before he could settle, a tall man with a carefully trimmed beard approached. "Malachi Brown," he introduced, extending a hand. "No relation, but we've got the same last name. Must be fate."

Hakeem returned the handshake. "Nice to meet you, man. You're the one running the place now?"

Malachi's grin widened. "Yep. Rochelle decided it was time to retire. I'm her nephew." He chuckled, then motioned toward the booth. "Go ahead and make yourself comfortable. I'll get someone to bring you a menu in a sec. Or if you already know what you want..."

"Menu's good," Hakeem said quietly. The swirl of voices around them fell to a soft hum; he could sense curious gazes from a few tables, but he ignored them. A tight coil of nerves still twisted in his stomach, a constant reminder of how vulnerable he felt. "Thanks."

Once Malachi left, Hakeem slid into the booth, mind racing. He was starving, but more than that, he was exhausted—physically and emotionally. He glanced around, remembering all the times he and Jada met up here after practice, splitting milkshakes or sneaking kisses when Rochelle's back was turned. Then, he'd been unstoppable, certain that the entire world lay at his feet.

He shut his eyes, letting a pang of regret wash over him. *I did what I thought was right.* That was his mantra after the breakup, and he'd clung to it like a life raft. But looking back, he realized how naive he'd been. All that talk about "protecting" each other by letting go... and he'd never asked what Jada truly wanted.

A soft voice broke into his thoughts: "Welcome to Rochelle's Old-Fashioned Diner. I'm Aimee—here's a menu. Can I get you something to drink while you decide?"

He glanced up to see a petite woman with a friendly smile. "Water's fine," he said, returning her smile politely.

She nodded. "Sure thing. If you're hungry, the chicken-and-waffles special is a hit today. Or you could try the new pumpkin bisque if you want something lighter."

Hakeem stared at her blankly for a second. "You know what, I'll do the chicken and waffles. I, uh... need some comfort food."

Aimee jotted it down. "Coming right up."

As she walked away, he let out a slow breath. Comfort food. Maybe that's what he needed—something warm and familiar to remind him he belonged. He was still swirling in thought, vaguely aware of the low chatter drifting between tables, when a snippet of conversation caught his attention.

"...didn't realize Jada Davis was back in town. She's working at the hospital, right?"

He froze. The faint clamoring of forks and plates vanished beneath the thunder of his heartbeat. *Jada's here.*

He'd known it was a possibility; gossip at Rashad's wedding suggested she might return. But hearing confirmation—hearing her name like that, so casually in the air—slammed into him like a linebacker. *She's actually here.*

His pulse hammered. Did she know he was back, too? How would she react if they crossed paths? *Would she hate me, or just feel nothing at all?*

Before he could process the swirling mess of questions, Aimee returned with his water, setting it down gently. "Your food should be out soon," she said, noticing the tension on his face. "Everything okay?"

"Yeah," he croaked, clearing his throat. "Fine. Just... adjusting."

She nodded sympathetically. "I get it. I'm fairly new here, too. Sweetgum can be overwhelming sometimes, but it's a good place if you give it a chance."

Hakeem managed a tight smile as she left. He laced his fingers together atop the table, focusing on the faint scars and calluses along his knuckles—remnants of countless hours gripping a football. The game that once defined him felt painfully distant, but not as distant as Jada.

She's here. The knowledge rattled him, awakening an old, raw longing he thought he'd buried. He could still see the heartbreak in her eyes on that final night. Could still feel her hand slipping out of his grasp. Could still hear her voice trembling with disbelief when he told her it was over.

And now? Now he had a bum knee, a half-finished NFL career, and a lifetime of regrets. He'd come home to Sweetgum hoping to find direction, maybe even find her. But fear twisted in his chest. She'd never forgive him, right?

His phone buzzed on the table, snapping him out of the spiral. The screen showed a missed call from his team's trainer, but he couldn't bring himself to listen to the voicemail. He had enough reminders of what he'd lost.

Not for the first time, he imagined Jada's reaction if they met. His heart pounded, caught between dread and desperate hope. He couldn't undo the past, but he had to believe there might be a future.

He sipped his water, the cool rush doing little to calm the storm inside him. He'd have to plan his next move carefully. If he wanted to see Jada again—if he wanted even the faintest chance of repairing what they'd once had—he couldn't barge in recklessly. He needed to think, to show her that this time, he was ready to be the man she deserved.

Because leaving her behind was the biggest regret of his life.

CHAPTER FOUR

On her first official day at Sweetgum Hospital, Jada walked the brightly lit hallway of the Physical Therapy wing with a folder clutched to her chest. Her white coat felt stiff on her shoulders—new and untested, just like the tiny surge of nerves dancing under her skin. She inhaled slowly, trying to settle the butterflies.

I'm a professional, she reminded herself. *I've got a doctorate in physical therapy. I'm here to help people.*

And she *did* want to help. She loved guiding patients through recovery, watching their bodies grow stronger one stretch at a time. In the hush of an exam room, she felt purposeful—like every day was a chance to offer someone a fresh start. That was her passion: giving others hope when they feared they'd lost it.

Except, as she reached the PT office, her resolve wobbled. Because right there, in the day's patient roster, she spotted a name that nearly made her heart drop to her ankles:

Hakeem Brown.

She'd known there was a chance she'd see him eventually, of course—Sweetgum was small, and gossip about Hakeem's injury trickled through the grapevine. But *today? Her first day?* Her pulse thundered. She scanned the rest of the schedule, as if double-checking for a possible misprint. Yet there it was, printed in crisp black letters.

For a moment, it felt like being eighteen again, knees trembling under the stadium lights as he said goodbye. The same ache flared in her chest. *Don't fall apart now,* she told herself. *You can handle this.*

She squeezed her eyes shut and drew in a calming breath. Her job demanded professionalism. And, if nothing else, she'd prove to *him*—and to herself—that she was no longer the broken girl he'd left behind.

"Dr. Davis?" came a voice from behind. It was Anne, the department coordinator, peering into the office with a friendly smile. "Your new patient's waiting in Room Six."

Jada's throat felt dry. "Room Six," she echoed, nodding. "Got it. Thank you."

Anne offered a short wave, then hurried off to wrangle another patient. Jada took a moment to flip through Hakeem's file, despite already suspecting what it would say: *ACL tear, subsequent surgical repair, significant risk for partial mobility loss if rehab is neglected.* The notes indicated he'd come from a top clinic in Atlanta—but now he wanted to continue his therapy here, back in Sweetgum.

Why, Hakeem? A swell of unanswered questions welled in her chest. Part of her wanted to march in and demand an explanation for why he'd decided to return. But that wasn't her role. She was his physical therapist, nothing more.

With trembling fingers, she smoothed down her coat and walked to Room Six. She paused outside the door, forcing her heart to calm. The hum of fluorescent lights buzzed overhead. *Professional,* she repeated mentally. *You can do this.*

One last breath. Then she pushed open the door.

The first thing she saw was his back—wide shoulders

hunched forward as he sat on the edge of the therapy table. Even though he was seated, she could tell he was tall, same as always. He wore a T-shirt and athletic shorts, revealing the defined lines of an athlete's build. A black knee brace clung to his left leg.

He glanced up at the sound of the door, and their eyes met.

Time twisted. Jada's heart lurched, an odd mixture of rage and longing spiraling through her. Seven years vanished in the space of a single second. He looked…older, yes, but still achingly handsome and familiar. Those dark eyes held the same flicker of vulnerability she'd seen that night he walked away.

"Jada," he breathed, rising partially from the table before hesitating, grimacing slightly when his knee protested.

"Mr. Brown," she said, voice taut, even as her heartbeat threatened to deafen her. She slipped into the clinical role like a shield, stepping forward to extend her hand. "I'm Dr. Davis. I'll be your physical therapist."

He swallowed, eyes clouded with something unreadable. "Dr. Davis," he repeated, as though trying to get used to the title. "I—I didn't know it would be you."

A flicker of bitterness prodded her chest. *Of course you didn't.* She forced a polite smile that barely curved her lips. "Small town. Surprises are bound to happen."

Hakeem's gaze lingered on her face, and she felt a tremor ripple through her composure. She reminded herself: *He's just another patient.* Even if her heart screamed otherwise.

Clearing her throat, she set the file on a small rolling table. "Let's talk about your injury history and goals for therapy. You can start by telling me about any lingering pain or stiffness."

She hated how robotic she sounded, but if she let her guard down, she wasn't sure if she'd scream or cry or both. Her pulse pounded so loudly that she almost missed his next words.

"I…hurt it pretty bad," Hakeem began, voice low. "ACL tear,

cartilage damage. Docs in Atlanta said I might not…might not play again."

There was a bleakness in his tone that chipped at her resolve. He was obviously in pain—both physical and emotional. She wanted to comfort him, to place a hand on his shoulder the way she would any other patient, but memories of heartbreak seared that impulse.

"We'll do what we can," she answered softly, meeting his gaze with professionalism rather than pity. "Our goal is maximum recovery, even if the NFL isn't on the table right now."

He flinched at the mention of the league, exhaling slowly. "Right. Of course."

For a heartbeat, neither spoke. Tension crackled between them, thick enough to taste. Jada fought the urge to look away, to shield herself from the questions swirling in his eyes. *Why are you here?* she wanted to ask. *Why did you come back?*

"Lie back, please," she managed instead, guiding him gently to a supine position on the table. "I need to check your range of motion, do some basic assessments."

He eased onto his back, wincing slightly as he moved his injured knee. She positioned herself at his side, setting one hand beneath his calf. Instantly, a jolt of awareness shot up her arm. His skin was warm, taut with tension—familiar, yet so far from the boy she'd known. Carefully, she lifted his leg and rotated gently, testing angles.

Hakeem's breathing hitched, whether from pain or something else, she couldn't tell. Her own breath felt unsteady, but she forced her focus on the job. She measured angles, noted tightness, mentally recorded how the injury had progressed.

"You're still swelling a bit around the joint," she said quietly, resting his leg on the table. "I'll give you some exercises to reduce that before we push further."

"Right," he muttered. "Whatever you say, Doc."

She straightened, stepping out of arm's reach. "We'll meet twice a week to start," she explained, flipping through a checklist. "I'll do my best to help you recover, but a lot depends on whether you follow the regimen outside these walls."

Hakeem nodded, gaze flicking to her face. "Jada—"

She held up a hand. "We'll keep this professional," she said, maybe too sharply. "Outside of these sessions, that's... I can't blur lines with a patient."

A flash of hurt crossed his features, and he swallowed. "Understood."

The pause that followed felt like a heavy weight. Part of her wanted to flee, hide from the look in his eyes—the same look that once made her heart sing. She stifled a tremor in her voice.

"I'll print out your initial exercises," she said, moving toward the computer in the corner. "After we're done, you can schedule your next appointment with the front desk."

Hakeem slowly sat up on the table. She refused to glance his way, keeping her eyes fixed on the screen as she typed. Out of the corner of her vision, she saw him rub the back of his neck, as if battling a million unspoken words.

When she finally handed him the printout, their fingers almost brushed. She snatched her hand back quickly, feeling her face heat. "Do you have any questions?"

He shook his head, staring at the paper. His voice was subdued. "No...not right now."

"Okay," she said briskly, forcing a tight smile. "Then I'll see you next session, Mr. Brown."

He left without another word. The door clicked shut, leaving her alone in the sterile stillness of the exam room. Jada closed her eyes, exhaling a shaky breath. The scent of antiseptic and floor polish surrounded her, but it couldn't scrub away the raw storm swirling inside her.

She'd thought she was prepared for this. But seeing him again hurt more than any old memory—and the worst part was how her heart still thudded with that stupid, stubborn hope she'd fought to bury years ago.

"Get it together," she murmured to herself. *Professional.* She'd chosen this path; she'd help him recover. But the part of her that never really healed whispered that therapy for a shattered knee was far easier than therapy for a shattered heart.

CHAPTER FIVE

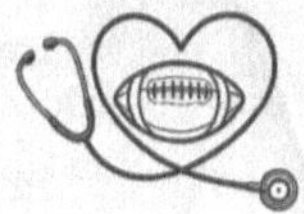

*H*akeem drove straight from the hospital to his family's dairy farm, the tension in his shoulders flaring with every mile. His mind wouldn't let go of that fleeting, tormenting moment with Jada. She'd been all business, her gaze clinical and guarded—and it sliced deeper than he thought possible.

Pulling up the dusty driveway, he parked beside the old barn and cut the engine. Late afternoon sunshine bathed the farm in a honeyed glow, illuminating the rows of cows in the adjacent field. He caught sight of Rashad, his older brother, near the fence. Rashad's tall frame was relaxed, arms folded as he chatted with one of the farmhands. When he spotted Hakeem, he raised a hand in greeting.

"How'd it go, little bro?" Rashad called, meeting Hakeem halfway between the truck and the barn. "You look like you've seen a ghost."

Hakeem tried to summon a reassuring grin, but it wavered. "More like someone I never stopped missing."

Rashad's expression shifted from casual to concerned. "You ran into Jada, didn't you?"

He nodded, his throat tight. "She's my physical therapist. I had no idea." Slowly, he rubbed at his knee, still throbbing from the session—and maybe from old heartache. "She's...changed, Rashad. Stronger, more distant. But I guess that's what happens when you walk away from someone."

They trudged toward the barn, the scent of hay and manure wrapping around them like an old blanket. Rashad paused at a stack of feed bags, resting one hand on a weather-worn post. "Look, I'm not gonna pretend to know what she's feeling. But I saw her right after you broke things off. She was wrecked, Hakeem. You can't expect her to welcome you back with open arms."

"I know," Hakeem muttered, guilt tightening his chest. "I'm not even sure if she'd want to talk outside therapy sessions. She made it clear we have to keep things professional."

"Can you blame her? She's gotta protect her heart." Rashad's tone was firm but not unkind. "Truth is, she deserves to see if you're serious—about being here and about rebuilding trust."

Hakeem swallowed the lump in his throat, memories of Jada's shuttered gaze flashing through his mind. "I am serious," he said quietly. "I just don't know how to show her. It's not like I can promise a bright NFL future anymore."

Rashad shook his head. "That was never all she cared about. You know that. She loved *you*, not your football career." He slung an arm around Hakeem's shoulders. "Maybe it's time you let her see who you are now—and stop hiding what you're feeling."

They made their way into the barn, where a few cows lowed softly, flicking their tails against the late-summer heat. Hakeem inhaled the familiar scent of grain and straw. He used to hate the farm as a teenager, itching to get away to bigger things. Now he found a strange peace here—some sense of belonging that had always been overshadowed by his dreams of stardom.

Rashad picked up a brush and began grooming one of the cows. "Start simple," he said over his shoulder. "You came back to Sweetgum for a reason, right? Show her you're not running this time. Keep at therapy. Let her see you trying, physically and otherwise. Don't push, but don't vanish."

Hakeem took the brush from Rashad and quietly helped. The repetitive strokes gave him something to focus on, taming the swirl of regrets in his head. "I just don't want to make her uncomfortable," he admitted. "She looked ready to bolt the second she saw me."

"She'll either warm up or tell you to get lost." Rashad turned, eyes intent. "But at least you'll know you tried. If there's anything left between you two, it won't just disappear because you're both scared."

Hakeem nodded, chest heavy yet somehow lighter at the same time. He thought of Jada's cool professionalism, the way her hand trembled just slightly when she touched his leg. She hadn't been indifferent—he could feel the tension crackling between them. That spark was real, no matter how hardened she seemed.

They finished brushing the cow, then stepped outside into the fading sunlight. A gentle breeze ruffled the tall grass. Rashad clapped him on the shoulder. "Come on, man. Let's get some dinner before I head home to India. You can stick around here tonight if you want, or head back to your apartment in town."

Hakeem pocketed his keys, feeling a hint of resolve settle in. "Thanks, bro. I'll grab something and crash here. I need to think —figure out how to move forward. Because I'm not letting Jada slip away again. Not without giving it everything I've got."

Rashad nodded, offering a small smile. "That's the spirit. Just remember, healing takes time. Yours, and hers."

Hakeem looked out over the rolling fields, the sun dipping behind the horizon in a fiery display. He recalled Jada's steady hands on his injured knee, her guarded eyes that once over-flowed with love for him. Guilt and yearning collided, but beneath it all, a fragile hope flickered.

He might not know his next play yet, but for the first time in a long while, he knew exactly what he wanted. And this time, he wasn't going to run.

CHAPTER SIX

*J*ada sat at her small desk in the physical therapy office, staring blankly at a report she was supposed to be typing. Despite her best efforts, her mind kept drifting back to the day before—back to Hakeem, lying on that exam table, shock and regret warring on his face. A tremor fluttered through her chest every time she remembered the quiet way he'd said her name.

"You okay, Dr. Davis?" asked a warm voice near the door.

She glanced up to see Anne, the department coordinator, with a gentle concern etched into her features. Jada forced a small smile. "Yeah, I'm fine. Just…settling in."

Anne nodded, sympathy in her eyes. "It can be tough starting somewhere new. You're doing great so far, though. The patients like you."

"Thanks," Jada murmured. She tried to muster more enthusiasm, but her heart wasn't in it. "I'll get these notes finished soon."

Once Anne left, Jada exhaled slowly. She'd spent half the night replaying that session with Hakeem. The old ache in her chest refused to subside, and even now, she couldn't help wondering if he was as shaken by their reunion as she was.

But she pushed the thought aside—she had a job to do. She typed furiously, summarizing the morning's sessions with other patients. Each word felt like a small victory over her spinning emotions. *Focus on your work. You're a professional.*

When lunchtime arrived, she grabbed her bag and hurried out, eager for a break from the sterile hush of the hospital corridors. A soft breeze brushed her cheeks as she stepped into the midday sun. Without much thought, she hopped into her car and drove down Main Street, heading straight for Rochelle's Old-Fashioned Diner.

The diner's windows glinted cheerfully in the light. Stepping inside, Jada let the warm scents of fried chicken and fresh cornbread envelop her. The place was bustling but cozy, customers chatting at tables while Malachi deftly took orders behind the counter.

"Jada!" A bubbly voice rang out.

She turned to see her old friend Aliyah waving from a corner booth. Aliyah grinned, baby carrier perched beside her. Sure enough, there was Aliyah's little one cooing softly, big round eyes taking in the diner's commotion.

Jada's heart lightened at the sight. She slid into the booth, letting out a sigh. "Hey, you. You look good. Marriage and motherhood seems to agree with you."

Aliyah rolled her eyes playfully. "You mean disheveled and covered in baby spit-up?" She reached over to smooth the infant's blanket. "I'll take the compliment, though. How've you been, Dr. Davis?"

"Busy," Jada said with a tight smile, nodding her thanks when Malachi briefly stopped by to drop off menus. "Thanks," she murmured to him, then turned back to Aliyah. "How's Chrysta doing? I heard she recently got married?" she said, attempting to divert attention from herself.

"She's doing great. Her husband Terrance owns the new bridal shop up the street. I fully take credit for that relationship since they got together trying to trick me," she laughed. Her eyes roamed Jada's face. "But seriously, how have you been?"

"I'm…adjusting."

Aliyah's gaze sharpened. "I heard from Mrs. Zhang that a certain NFL star came in for physical therapy."

Jada's stomach twisted. Of course word had traveled already; small-town grapevines had always been unstoppable. "News travels fast, doesn't it?"

"Faster than you think," Aliyah agreed, resting a hand on Jada's. "So…how are you? Really?"

A thousand emotions vied for control. Jada swallowed, forcing a steady tone. "I'm fine. I can handle it. Hakeem is just another patient, and I'm a professional."

Aliyah's eyes narrowed with gentle skepticism. "Girl, you were wrecked when he left. The entire senior class knew how serious you two were. Are you sure you're okay?"

Jada fiddled with a napkin, eyes dropping to the table. "He caught me off-guard. I told him we'd keep things strictly professional, which is good. I—I can't risk my career over personal baggage."

Aliyah squeezed her hand. "That's fair. But Jada, ignoring what you feel won't make it disappear."

A pinch of frustration stabbed Jada's chest. "What do you want me to do? Throw myself at him again? He made his choice a long time ago. He left me. I'm not… I won't put my heart on the line just because he's waltzed back into town."

Aliyah nodded slowly. "I'm not saying you should. Just… don't bottle it up. You'll have to work through those feelings at some point."

Before Jada could respond, Aimee popped by with a friendly smile, setting down two glasses of iced tea. "On the house," she said. "Let me know if you need any recommendations."

"Thanks," Jada replied, grateful for the interruption.

A few minutes later, she settled on a grilled chicken sandwich—something simple and quick—while Aliyah ordered fries to share. As they waited, Jada finally allowed herself a small venting session. She explained in hushed tones how she'd felt standing next to Hakeem, how her heart pounded even though she resented him for the past.

"I hate that he can still do this to me," she muttered. "Like, I was finally moving on. I have goals, a career path."

Aliyah listened, occasionally offering a nod or a sympathetic smile. When the food arrived, Jada took a bite of her sandwich, chewing mechanically. She barely tasted the savory marinade because her mind spun with thoughts of the next therapy session.

"Maybe you should consider referring him to another therapist," Aliyah suggested gently. "You don't have to treat him."

Jada twisted her napkin. "I thought about that, but it feels like...like I'd be letting him push me out again. This is *my* job. I can handle it."

Aliyah studied her face. "Just make sure you're not hurting yourself in the process. You don't owe him anything."

"I know," Jada murmured. But a small voice in her head whispered that she *did* owe it to herself to see this through. Maybe confronting Hakeem—day after day, session after session—would force her to finally lay the past to rest. She couldn't keep running from him forever, not in this town.

They finished eating, and Jada felt a slight ease in her chest, like a valve releasing pent-up pressure. Talking to Aliyah always helped. The baby gurgled happily, drawing a soft coo from Jada, and for a fleeting moment, she imagined what life might have been like if things had turned out differently—if she and Hakeem had stayed together, built a life here in Sweetgum. Would they have children of their own? She quickly shoved the thought aside.

Aliyah paid for her meal—despite Jada's protest—and they parted ways at the diner's entrance, embracing warmly. "Thanks for letting me unload," Jada said, genuine gratitude filling her voice.

"Anytime." Aliyah kissed the baby's forehead. "And I mean it, Jada: protect your heart. If it gets too hard, pass him off. No shame in that."

Jada merely nodded, stepping into the bright midday sun. She took a moment to fill her lungs with fresh air. Aliyah's advice echoed in her mind, but she couldn't shake the stubborn determination taking root in her gut.

I'm not running, she decided.

Adjusting her purse on her shoulder, she headed back to the hospital, resolved to face Hakeem head-on—whatever that might cost her heart.

CHAPTER SEVEN

*H*akeem parked his pickup on the grass near the back of the old high school stadium, the place that once echoed with his every victory cheer. Leaning against the tailgate, he surveyed the empty bleachers and the worn track, each detail stirring memories of the boy he used to be.

He'd spent the morning helping Rashad on the farm, but his thoughts kept drifting back to Jada. Even the soothing rhythm of farm chores hadn't stopped the reel of yesterday's therapy session from playing in his mind. Her professionalism. Her guarded eyes. The brief tremor in her hand when she touched his knee.

You can't force this, he reminded himself, repeating Rashad's words. But he also knew he couldn't sit idle and hope for magic. If he wanted any shot at redeeming himself in Jada's eyes, he had to start somewhere.

And so he came here—to the place where a teenage Hakeem first realized he could soar, and also the place where he'd last held Jada close before that final, fateful breakup. Standing on the patchy grass, he tried not to flinch at the swirl of memories:

cheering crowds, Jada's laughter, the weight of a diploma in one hand and her heart in the other.

He limped a few steps along the fifty-yard line, feeling the tug on his knee brace. The ache in his joint told him he should be careful—should probably be doing the exercises Jada gave him. But his spirit needed this moment, needed to confront what once was.

Lost in thought, he didn't notice the approach of an older man with a whistle around his neck until he was nearly at Hakeem's shoulder.

"Coach Jones?" Hakeem said, startled. He hadn't seen his old football coach in years.

The gray-haired coach smiled wide, lines crinkling at his eyes. "Figured that was you, boy. Heard you were back. Sorry about your injury."

Hakeem nodded, swallowing a wave of emotion. "Thanks. It's...rough."

Coach looked out over the field. "Guess you're here to remember the glory days?"

A sad laugh escaped Hakeem's throat. "Something like that."

They stood in companionable silence, the wind stirring the tall grass at the field's edge. Finally, Coach Jones cleared his throat. "You know, you had a gift, Hakeem. Quick reflexes, a strategic mind... But I always thought your real advantage was that big heart of yours."

Hakeem scoffed lightly. "Didn't feel so big when I left Jada behind."

Coach's gaze sharpened. "Not my place to pry, but I could see how close you two were. Hate to see something like that end."

Hakeem studied the empty bleachers. "It ended because I thought it was best for both of us. But now, seeing her again..." He shook his head. "I realize how badly I hurt her."

Coach folded his arms. "If she meant that much, then she

probably still does. Question is, are you willing to do the work to fix things?"

Hakeem blew out a breath, the truth of that statement pressing on his chest. *Do the work.* That was exactly what Jada deserved—someone ready to put in effort, someone who wouldn't walk away when it got hard. "I am," he said quietly. "But I don't know if she'll give me a chance."

"She might not. But if you care about her, you'll try anyway."

Hakeem stared down at the grass, replaying Jada's face from the therapy session. The guarded pain behind her eyes burned in his memory. "I have a second appointment in a few days," he said, voice hushed. "I want her to see I'm here for real this time. Not just counting the days 'til I can leave again."

"Then show her," Coach said simply.

They exchanged a few more words, reminiscing about old games and the changing face of Sweetgum High. Then Coach gave him a hearty clap on the shoulder and strolled away, leaving Hakeem alone at midfield. A hush settled over the empty stadium, and for a moment, he imagined the roar of a crowd—cheering not just for a touchdown, but maybe for him finding the courage to make amends.

He bent, gingerly stretching his leg. His knee complained, but he breathed through the discomfort. *I'll keep at the exercises,* he promised himself, *not just because I might play again someday— but because I want to be stronger for her, too.*

The sun dipped lower, casting long shadows across the field. Hakeem lingered until the cool breeze set goosebumps along his arms. Finally, he trudged back to his truck. As he pulled away, he glanced in the rearview mirror at the silent bleachers fading behind him.

He might not have a clear playbook for winning back Jada's trust, but for the first time since returning to Sweetgum, he felt a glimmer of purpose. All he could do now was show up—again and again—until maybe, just maybe, she believed in him once more.

CHAPTER EIGHT

*J*ada stifled a yawn, rubbing the bridge of her nose as she surveyed her schedule for the day. The clock on the wall read ten-thirty, and she'd already powered through two patient sessions. She knew who was up next—*Hakeem Brown, second appointment.* Her pulse quickened at the thought.

She opened the door to the small staff lounge. The smell of stale coffee and disinfectant wrapped around her. Taking a moment to refill her mug, she listened to hushed conversations from passing nurses. She caught fragments of phrases—something about a newborn, something about a complex surgery—but her mind was stuck on the swirl of conflicting emotions that always appeared whenever she thought of Hakeem.

You can handle this, she reminded herself. She'd gotten through the first session, and despite the lingering ache in her chest, she'd maintained control. *Professional.* That was the word she kept clutching to, like a lifeline.

With a deep breath, she headed back to her office and found him already there in the waiting area, knee brace partially hidden beneath athletic shorts. His gaze lifted the moment she stepped through the door. For a split second, neither moved—just two people with an entire world of unfinished business between them.

"Hi," she managed, injecting a brisk efficiency into her tone. "Ready?"

He nodded, standing up carefully. "Yeah…ready."

She led him down the hall to a private therapy room, her heart thudding a touch harder than she liked. Inside, she motioned to the table, setting her coffee aside before flipping through his chart on a metal stand.

"How'd the exercises go?" she asked, purposely cool. "Any increased pain or unusual swelling after you tried them?"

A faint smile ghosted his mouth. "No more than expected. I did everything on your printout." He tapped the brace. "Hurt at first, but it's getting a little easier."

She nodded, scribbling notes. "Good. Consistency is key." Then, setting the chart aside, she studied him. "Let's see your range of motion today. Lie back, please."

He followed her instructions, stretching out on the table. She took a moment to check his brace. Their gazes flicked to each other, tangling briefly. She wished desperately she could be numb to that spark, but it was there—low and tense in the air, just like old times.

She gently lifted his leg, testing angles. "How's that?"

A quiet hiss escaped him. "Hurts… but not unbearable."

She nodded, pressing a hand to the side of his knee, feeling for swelling. "We'll do gentle stretches, then some light exercises if you can handle it." She moved around to face him and noticed the tightness in his jaw. "We'll go slow, okay?"

His eyes locked on hers. "I trust you."

Those three words made her chest constrict. She swallowed, forcing the reminder that this was a patient-therapist scenario —nothing more. He might trust her, but she didn't trust him.

He'd broken her trust seven years ago. "All right. On three," she said softly, and guided his leg outward.

He grimaced, grip tightening on the edges of the therapy table. She held steady, counting seconds, keeping her focus on the precise angle of his leg. When she finished the stretch, he exhaled slowly, and she could practically feel the tension radiating off him—both physical and emotional.

"You're doing well," she said, stepping back. "Short rests between sets."

He propped himself on his elbows, an unreadable expression on his face. "Jada… thanks. For this."

She forced a polite nod. "I'm just doing my job."

His gaze dipped, and for a moment, it seemed he was bracing to say something more personal. But he hesitated, pressing his lips together.

She cleared her throat, forging ahead. "Let's try a quick warm-up on the stationary bike before we move into strength training. But nothing too strenuous—you're still early in your recovery."

Hakeem slid carefully off the table and followed her to the corner where a compact exercise bike stood near a row of dumbbells. Jada showed him the adjustments for seat height, her fingers fluttering over levers and knobs with professional ease. She tried not to notice how close he stood, the warmth of his presence igniting unwelcome nostalgia.

Once he was settled, he started pedaling slowly. She crossed her arms, studying his form. "Let me know if you feel any sharp pain."

He nodded, keeping his gaze focused on the pedals for a few rotations. When he finally spoke, his voice was low. "It's so weird being the one *needing* help. You know I used to be a star athlete—"

She arched a brow. "I know."

A humorless chuckle slipped out. "Right. You know better than anyone. It's just… everything's different now."

She wasn't sure how to respond. *Was he fishing for pity? Or just trying to open a dialogue they'd never finished?* The tension in the room pressed on her sternum.

"Life happens," she said carefully, keeping her tone as neutral as possible. "You adapt."

He glanced up, eyes searching her face. "I guess so. I'm just trying to figure out what to do next. Hard to imagine what life looks like without football."

Her heart twisted with an odd mixture of sympathy and the sting of old wounds. She remembered how *football* had been the biggest thing he prioritized back then. She remembered how that dream overshadowed *them.* Still, she couldn't stop the flicker of empathy that ignited—she knew exactly how it felt to lose a path you believed was your future.

He rode on in silence for another minute. Jada stepped in, adjusting the resistance slightly. "Tell me if that's too much."

"It's fine," he murmured. After a few more turns of the pedals, he slowed. "You've changed, Jada."

Her spine stiffened. "I've grown up, Hakeem. That's what people do."

A shadow of regret passed over his face. "I see that. Back then, I… I guess I never realized what I was losing." He rubbed a hand over his brace, eyes darting away. "You're good at this. The therapy, I mean. You really care about your patients."

She inhaled sharply, caught between the urge to thank him and the urge to tell him to leave those memories buried. Settling for a clipped nod, she said, "I do care. That's why I became a therapist—to help people get back on their feet."

"And you're good at it," he repeated, voice softer now. "I'm not surprised."

A swirl of anger and sorrow churned inside her. She didn't want his praise. She wanted answers to questions she'd buried—

Why wasn't I enough? Why did you decide for both of us? But she couldn't ask any of that, not here. So she refocused on the session, adjusting the bike once more and checking her watch.

"All right," she said. "That's enough for now." She gestured for him to stop. "Time for some strength-building exercises."

He eased off, wincing slightly as he stood. She moved to support him, but he steadied himself without her help. Then he glanced at her, a rueful half-smile tugging at his lips. "Sorry," he muttered. "Don't mean to be a downer."

She pressed her lips together. "Let's just keep it professional, okay? We've got a job to do—both of us."

Hakeem's shoulders slumped. "Right. I understand."

Swiftly, she guided him through a series of low-resistance exercises—simple lifts, step-ups, mini-squats with a stability ball. He gritted his teeth through the discomfort, sweat gathering at his temples. Despite the thick haze of unresolved emotions between them, she couldn't help admiring his effort. This was a side of Hakeem she always respected: his drive, his commitment to pushing past limits.

"Good," she said at last, handing him a towel. "That's enough for today."

He wiped his forehead, breathing hard. "Thanks."

Jada collected her clipboard, scribbling quick notes about his session. She avoided looking at him. "I'll see you in a few days. Same time."

He started to say something, but his phone buzzed in his pocket. Fishing it out, he grimaced at the screen. "I... uh, yeah. Same time," he muttered. "See you then, Doc."

"Bye," she said, voice cool. He hobbled toward the door, brace catching slightly on the threshold.

When he was gone, Jada slowly exhaled, sinking onto the nearest chair. Her stomach felt knotted, and her heart thumped like it was caught in a vise. She'd held herself together, kept her professional veneer—but the confrontation with the boy she once loved, the man he'd become, was tearing at her composure.

She pressed a hand to her chest, fighting back the wave of confusion. She wasn't sure if she was proud for standing firm or devastated by the distance she was forcing. Perhaps both.

Glancing down at the list of notes she'd taken about his performance, she ran a finger over his name. *Hakeem Brown. The one who gave up on us.* She'd built her entire adult life on not needing him, on forging her own path. Now her world had realigned, yanking her heart in directions she thought she'd left behind.

Focus, she told herself. *You can't fall apart.*

It was a mantra she'd have to repeat over and over—every single time she faced him again. Because the next time wouldn't be any easier, and the past refused to let go.

CHAPTER NINE

$\mathcal{H}$akeem stepped through the familiar doorway of Rochelle's Old-Fashioned Diner, a twinge in his knee reminding him to slow his pace. The afternoon sun filtering through the big windows lit up the checkered floors with a cozy glow. Even though the diner was busy, a hush fell over several tables as folks glanced in his direction. Some gave small nods or friendly waves; others studied him like a curiosity returned home.

Small town indeed, he thought ruefully. Yet a part of him appreciated that sense of belonging he'd once scoffed at.

Spotting an empty stool at the counter, he eased himself onto it, ignoring the tight pull in his knee brace. Aimee, the petite woman in an apron, appeared behind the counter with a bright smile.

"Hey there, Hakeem. Need a menu?"

He shook his head. "Just a sweet tea. Maybe a piece of peach cobbler if you've got some left."

Aimee laughed lightly. "Always. Malachi's in the back, but I'll let him know you're here. Haven't seen you around in a minute."

"Been busy." *Thinking about Jada*— But he didn't add that.

While Aimee fetched his order, Hakeem drummed his fingers on the counter. He replayed the morning's session with Jada, every exchange crackling with tension. Her professional demeanor was admirable, but it left him feeling shut out, like he was the last person in the world she wanted to see. And maybe he was. In truth, he didn't blame her. After what he did to her it was a miracle she'd agreed to treat him. But it hurt. Still, he couldn't feel sorry for himself because, in reality, he'd caused this pain for himself and for her.

"Hey, man!" Malachi's voice interrupted Hakeem's thoughts. Rochelle's nephew emerged from the kitchen wearing a tidy button-down and an easy grin. He extended a hand, which Hakeem shook. "How's that knee?"

Hakeem lifted a shoulder. "Coming along, I guess. Jada's tough on me."

Malachi arched an eyebrow, catching the undercurrent in Hakeem's tone. "That's good, right? You want a therapist who won't let you slack off."

Hakeem managed a half-smile. "Yeah. She definitely doesn't let me off the hook."

Aimee slid the sweet tea and cobbler in front of Hakeem. He thanked her softly, then sampled the warm dessert—its sugary aroma comforting, a reminder of simpler days.

As Malachi stayed nearby, organizing supplies behind the counter, Hakeem mustered the nerve to speak up. "Hey, can I ask you something?"

"Sure." Malachi paused, propping an elbow on the gleaming countertop.

Hakeem hesitated. He wasn't used to laying out his personal drama so openly. But he needed an outside perspective. "You... um, you got together with Aimee, right? I heard some bits of that story. You guys overcame a lot to make it work."

Malachi's lips twitched in a smile as he cast a brief look at Aimee. She was helping another customer, far enough away to give them privacy. "Yeah, it took time. We had a few hiccups—misunderstandings, secrets—but we pushed through them once we started being honest with each other."

Hakeem nodded slowly, mind drifting to Jada's stoic expressions and the walls she'd built. "I guess it's easier said than done, huh?"

Malachi's gaze was thoughtful. "It is. But if you really want someone in your life, you can't let fear keep you from trying. Gotta prove you're willing to do the work."

Hakeem snorted softly. "That's exactly what my brother said, in fewer words. I'm just not sure how to do that without pushing Jada away more. She's barely tolerant of me as a patient."

Malachi leaned on the counter. "Sometimes, it's about the small gestures. She's already forced to see you in therapy, so don't corner her with heavy conversations right now. Show her you're serious by being consistent, respectful. Maybe you find ways to help around town, be part of the community."

Aimee popped over, wiping her hands on a towel. "Exactly," she chimed in. "I didn't trust Malachi at first either, but then I saw he wasn't just talking—he was showing me who he was, day after day." She winked at Malachi, who chuckled.

Hakeem mulled that over, stirring the ice in his sweet tea. "So…like volunteering at events, or helping out with local stuff? Just…being present?"

"Sure," Malachi agreed. "Sweetgum's always got something going on. And if Jada sees you doing more than just rehabbing your knee—if she sees you investing in this place—she might realize you're not the same guy who left."

Hakeem's gaze dropped to his cobbler. *Investing in this place.* The idea jolted him. For so long, football was his entire world;

even after returning, he hadn't considered how he fit into Sweetgum's day-to-day life. But maybe that was the key. He could find a foothold here, prove he wasn't just idling until his next big break.

"Yeah," he said quietly, lifting his eyes to meet theirs. "I think that might help."

Aimee smiled. "Good. And you've got family here—Rashad, the dairy farm. People know your name, so maybe they'll welcome you if you put yourself out there."

Hakeem managed a grateful smile. "Thanks, both of you. I appreciate it."

He finished his cobbler in thoughtful silence. The plan settled in his mind: he'd show up around town, help out, maybe even sign up for a local project. The more he showed he cared about Sweetgum Meadows, the less it might seem like he was just passing through. Maybe word would reach Jada; maybe she'd catch glimpses of him blending into the community.

After paying, he gave Malachi and Aimee a grateful nod and headed for the door. Just as he stepped outside, a familiar voice called from behind him.

"Wait—Hakeem?"

He turned to see Aliyah, Jada's old friend, standing near the diner's entrance with a baby carrier in tow. His pulse stumbled. He barely knew Aliyah, but if anyone had Jada's ear, it was her.

She eyed him warily. "Didn't expect to see you here."

He cleared his throat, adjusting the brace peeking from his shorts. "Yeah, well… I'm back in town. Getting therapy at the hospital."

Aliyah's gaze flicked to his knee, then back to his face. "I know." She paused, shifting the baby carrier to her other arm. The infant cooed softly. "Jada's told me about your sessions."

A ripple of guilt and worry shot through him. "I'm sure she had plenty to say."

Aliyah's expression was guarded. "She's hurting, Hakeem. And she's worked really hard to build a life after…everything."

He swallowed, chest tight. "I know. I don't want to hurt her again."

Aliyah studied him for a moment, as if gauging his sincerity. Finally, she nodded. "If you're serious about making amends, you better be patient. She's not the same girl you left behind."

"I realize that," he said softly. "And I don't expect anything. I just…" He struggled for the right words. "I just want her to know I'm not running away again. Even if that means all I can do is say I'm sorry and let her live her life."

A hint of sympathy crept into Aliyah's features, though she kept her stance firm. "Fine. Just remember, one apology won't fix years of pain. And don't push her."

"I won't," he promised, voice tight.

She studied him another beat. Then the baby fussed, drawing her attention. "All right. I've gotta head in—this little one needs a feeding."

He stepped aside, allowing her to pass. "Right. Take care."

A ghost of a smile touched her lips, and she disappeared inside.

Hakeem exhaled, shoulders tense. That brief exchange felt like walking a tightrope—one wrong move, and he'd lose any chance of bridging the gap with Jada. But maybe there was a crack in the door, a faint sliver of hope that Aliyah wouldn't block him from trying.

He glanced down Main Street, the afternoon sun glinting against storefront windows. Something in him stirred—a determination to live up to the words he'd told Aliyah, to prove he was here to stay, for better or worse.

He'd start small, just as Malachi suggested. Help folks, show up for events, be a consistent presence in the life he once abandoned. If that was all he could do, he'd do it wholeheartedly, praying that, in time, Jada might see a version of him worthy of her forgiveness.

With that resolve anchored in his chest, Hakeem slid into his truck and drove off, the quaint heart of Sweetgum Meadows fading in the rearview mirror. But this time, he wasn't leaving—he was preparing to truly come home.

CHAPTER TEN

A week later, Jada found herself standing beneath the old gazebo in the heart of Sweetgum's town square, the warm sun filtering through the overhead lattice. Around her, a handful of volunteers sorted boxes, organized snacks, and prepared for the local Community Health Fair—an annual event intended to promote wellness and raise funds for hospital initiatives.

Jada took a moment to soak in the scene: residents milling about cheerily, strings of bunting fluttering overhead, and tables lined with flyers about nutrition and exercise. A pang of nostalgia tugged at her. She remembered seeing this fair years ago, when she and Hakeem would roam from booth to booth, munching samples of healthy snacks and snickering over the "boring adult stuff."

Her heart squeezed at the memory—one more reminder of what they'd lost. *Focus on now,* she reminded herself, squaring her shoulders. She had agreed to handle a booth about injury prevention and rehab, and she was determined to do it well, personal baggage aside.

"Jada!" called Anne, the hospital coordinator, from across the square. "Can you help move these pamphlets? We need extra copies at the main booth."

She nodded, marching over to retrieve an armload of bright brochures. "Coming!"

She maneuvered carefully through the growing crowd, depositing the materials on a small table near the entrance. As she straightened, the chatter around her seemed to fade. Her gaze locked onto a figure standing by the water station—tall, athletic, wearing a Sweetgum volunteer T-shirt that stretched over familiar broad shoulders.

Hakeem.

Her stomach dipped as she realized he was volunteering—she hadn't expected to see him here. Yet, as her eyes lingered on him, she couldn't tear them away. His athletic build was as fine as ever, every muscle and sinew bore witness to the discipline of his workout regimen, but now there was an added layer of maturity—a resolute, commanding handsomeness born of age and experience. Seven years ago, at eighteen, he'd been handsome in a boyish, vibrant way; now, he had grown into a man whose presence seemed both powerful and tender. She felt a bitter pang of resentment for not sharing in that transformation, for having been left behind as he evolved into the man he was today.

He moved methodically, sorting bottled water into neat rows while occasionally flashing a polite smile at passersby. Every so often, his braced knee forced him to pause, but he simply shifted his weight with quiet determination, resuming his work as though nothing could slow him down. In that moment, the mix of admiration and regret in her chest was almost overwhelming—he had taken that opportunity away from her, and now, witnessing his evolution from the vibrant boy of their youth to the distinguished man before her, she could not look away.

As she continued to watch him, something warm and hesitant stirred in her. She watched him greet an elderly woman with unhurried kindness, gently placing a bottle in her hands as though it were the most important act in the world. *He's really... helping.*

She tore her gaze away, biting back the swirl of memories. *Don't be naïve,* she told herself. Even if he was helping here, he'd made it very clear that he wanted nothing to do with her.

"Thanks for your help, Jada," Anne said as Jada rejoined her. "We've got a good turnout this year. Think you're ready to talk to folks about PT?"

Jada forced her thoughts back to the present. "Absolutely." She inhaled, setting her shoulders and heading to her booth, determined to focus on educating visitors about exercise programs and injury prevention.

And for a while, she managed. She answered questions about posture, demonstrated simple stretches, and offered pamphlets on hospital services. A steady stream of residents swung by—some older folks with nagging aches, a few athletes wanting tips on better training, and parents wrangling energetic kids.

Yet every few minutes, her eyes drifted to where Hakeem stood, greeting volunteers, hauling boxes, or helping direct someone to the right booth. He never tried to approach her, almost as if he'd sensed she needed space. Curiosity and caution warred in her chest.

Eventually, the midday heat swelled. Beads of sweat dotted her forehead. She stepped out from behind her booth to restock water cups for the demonstration table, and that's when she turned and found Hakeem there—holding out a fresh, cool bottle of water for her.

She froze, heart pounding at the kindness in his eyes. "Uh... thanks," she mumbled, retrieving the bottle.

"No problem," he said softly. His voice held none of the old cocky edge, just a quiet sincerity. "Figured you might need a break."

She nodded, taking a sip, fully aware of how her hand shook slightly. "Didn't realize you'd be volunteering."

He ran a hand over his hair, gaze flicking around the bustling square. "I heard they needed help, and I...I wanted to pitch in."

Jada swallowed, noticing how carefully he avoided stepping too close, as if determined not to crowd her. "Well, it's a good cause," she managed, fighting the mixture of resentment and reluctant admiration swirling in her gut.

They stood in silence for a moment, the festival's noise swirling around them: children laughing, a local band tuning instruments, adults chatting about upcoming events.

"Your booth looks popular," he remarked, gesturing to the line of people near the PT display. "They're lucky to have you here."

She rolled her lips together, not sure how to respond. Part of her wanted to snap that she'd always been capable of doing big things, with or without him. Another part softened at the earnest tone in his voice.

"I'm just giving advice," she said, glancing at her booth. "It's what I'm trained to do."

Hakeem nodded. "Yeah. And you're great at it—"

She bristled, placing a careful lid on the emotions clawing at her chest. "Listen, I appreciate the water," she said, voice stiffer than she intended. "But I should get back. I—there are people waiting."

"Sure," he replied quietly, stepping back to give her space. "Keep up the good work, Doc."

The nickname scratched at her heart, but she turned and walked away. Her pulse raced, torn between the comfort of his presence and the raw sting of the past.

Back at her booth, she forced a bright smile and continued her demonstrations, focusing on each visitor's questions. Still, the awareness of Hakeem lingered, a weight that refused to lift from her mind. Each time she glanced his way, he seemed genuinely immersed in helping others—fetching supplies, guiding a lost guest toward the right station, or steadying an older man's walker when it threatened to slip on the grass.

She didn't want to be impressed, yet she couldn't deny a grudging respect. *He's making an effort.*

When the fair began winding down, Jada's shoulders ached from hours of standing and talking. She stretched, massaging a tight spot in her neck. That's when she noticed a small commotion near a first-aid tent—an older woman had tripped, dropping a heavy box of brochures on her foot. Jada hurried over, her PT instincts kicking in.

"Oh dear," the woman gasped, tears in her eyes. "I think I twisted my ankle."

"Let me see," Jada soothed, kneeling to gently assess the woman's foot, aware of the crowd gathering. "Does this hurt?"

The woman winced with a nod. Jada looked around, realizing she'd need help elevating the ankle. But before she could call for a volunteer, Hakeem was there, quietly pressing a foam cushion into her free hand to prop up the woman's foot.

Their gazes met. She offered a hesitant nod of thanks, guiding the injured woman to rest on the cushion. "We'll need some ice and a wrap," she said, then paused, overwhelmed by the onlookers.

"I'll get it," Hakeem said, already heading for the supply table. Moments later, he returned with a reusable ice pack and an elastic bandage. Jada carefully iced the woman's ankle, instructing her on how to compress the area without cutting off circulation. Meanwhile, Hakeem knelt on the other side, ensuring the woman remained steady.

Within minutes, the worst of the pain eased, and the woman breathed a shaky sigh of relief. "Thank you," she whispered to them both, eyes glistening with gratitude.

"It's okay," Jada said gently. "You'll probably want to follow up with a doctor if swelling persists, but keep it iced and elevated for now."

Hakeem helped the woman shift onto a nearby folding chair, making sure she was stable before straightening. Jada stood as well, brushing grass off her jeans. Their eyes locked again—an echo of shared concern rippling between them.

"Nice work," he said softly.

Jada inhaled, the hint of warmth in his voice nudging at her defenses. "You too," she replied, guarded but genuine.

They parted ways soon after, each returning to their tasks as the fair concluded. Jada couldn't shake the sense that the inter-action, brief as it was, felt different—like they were acting as a team, even for a fleeting moment. *Almost like old times, before everything fell apart.*

But the ache in her chest refused to vanish. She gathered her booth materials, reminding herself that trust wasn't rebuilt in a single day, no matter how helpful he'd been. The wound he left in her life was too deep for quick fixes.

Still, as she packed up, she caught herself stealing glances at Hakeem. He was rolling up a tablecloth, his expression calm and focused. She could sense his awareness of her, but neither made a move to bridge the distance.

Perhaps that was how it needed to be right now—a slow dance of caution and tentative goodwill. The day's events soft-ened something in her heart, but the scars remained.

And for the first time, she realized that maybe, just maybe, she wasn't the only one carrying regrets about the past.

CHAPTER ELEVEN

Jada sat at her desk in the Physical Therapy wing, clicking through patient notes with meticulous care. A fresh wave of determination fueled her today—perhaps lingering from the community health fair, where she and Hakeem had shared a rare, cooperative moment. She wouldn't call it a breakthrough, but it was... something.

A soft knock at her door made her turn. Anne, the department coordinator, peeked in. "Hey, Dr. Davis, got a quick request: a patient in the general ward is having trouble with mobility exercises. Think you can consult for a minute?"

"Sure." Jada rose, grabbing her clipboard. "Lead the way."

They exited the therapy wing and turned down a corridor lined with large windows. Afternoon light spilled onto the polished floors, highlighting patients and visitors milling about. Jada mentally prepared for a routine consult: she'd assess the patient, recommend some adjustments, and head back to her desk. Simple enough.

But when they reached the general ward, she stopped short. Through the open door of a semi-private room, she glimpsed

Hakeem by a bed, speaking quietly with a teenage boy in a cast. Her heart gave an odd flutter.

"…just keep at it, man," Hakeem was saying gently. "You'll be back on the field before you know it. I'm proof that injuries don't have to end your world."

The kid smiled weakly, eyes lighting up at the sight of a bona fide NFL player—even if that player was currently sidelined. Jada pressed herself discreetly against the wall, uncertain whether to interrupt. Evidently, this wasn't a scheduled PT session. *What is he doing here?*

Anne cleared her throat softly beside her. "He asked if he could visit the pediatric ward. Thought maybe talking to another young athlete could help morale."

Jada swallowed, her throat suddenly tight. She'd heard rumors around the hospital that Hakeem had been coming in, volunteering his time. She just hadn't witnessed it firsthand.

The teen, who had bandaged ribs along with a cast on his left arm, nodded eagerly. "Thanks for talking to me, Mr. Brown. You, uh…you'll still be playing, right?"

Hakeem hesitated—just a flicker of uncertainty passing over his face. "Well, I'm working hard at rehab. Might take a while, but I'm not giving up."

The boy's eyes shone with admiration. "That's awesome." He glanced around. "I…wish I could keep practicing. My team is in the middle of playoffs."

Hakeem clapped him gently on the shoulder, mindful of the IV line. "Focus on healing. The rest will follow."

Something in Jada's chest twisted. This was a side of Hakeem she hadn't seen since high school: encouraging, patient, giving his time to someone else's recovery. She steeled her posture, remembering how easy it was to fall for the man who wore his heart on his sleeve.

Stepping forward, she softly rapped on the door frame. "Knock, knock."

Hakeem turned, his gaze catching hers. Surprise flickered in his expression, followed by warmth that he seemed to quickly school into politeness. "Hey, Doc."

She gave a curt nod. "I'm here for a consult." Her eyes shifted to the teen, who blinked in shy curiosity. "You must be Jeremy. I heard you've got some mobility concerns?"

Jeremy nodded, a bit star-struck to see them both. "Yeah. My arm's in a cast, and they said I might need therapy once it's off."

Jada crossed to the bed, slipping into her professional tone. "Let's see." She examined the cast's position. "Keep your fingers wiggling so the joints don't get stiff. We'll do simple exercises once it's removed, things like gentle rotations, grip strengtheners… We want to maintain as much function as possible."

She realized Hakeem was watching closely, almost as if he were learning from her. The attention made her pulse flutter, but she focused on the patient. "For now, listen to your doctors about rest and avoid bearing weight on that arm. The ribs need time, too."

Jeremy nodded earnestly. "Yes, ma'am."

Anne signaled that she needed Jada elsewhere, and Jada reached to pat Jeremy's good hand. "I'll check in again soon."

She turned to leave, brushing past Hakeem. He gave her a grateful half-smile, but didn't speak. His expression held a quiet respect that both unsettled and comforted her. Leaving the room, Jada tried to ignore how his presence caused her heart to pound.

A HALF-HOUR LATER, Jada wrapped up her consult in a different patient's room. On her way back to the therapy wing, she nearly collided with Hakeem in the hallway.

"Whoa," he murmured, stepping back so she wouldn't trip. "Sorry."

She steadied herself, smoothing her coat. "No harm done."

They stood there, hospital bustle swirling around. For a moment, she wondered if she should just walk away. But curiosity—and something deeper—prompted her to speak.

"You've been volunteering here?"

A hint of sheepishness crossed his face. "Yeah. Figured it couldn't hurt to give back, you know? If I can't be on the field, might as well help in other ways."

Jada studied him. She remembered the unstoppable confidence he once exuded, the relentless ambition that drove him to leave her behind. This new humility... Well, it tugged at her defenses, even as she tried to keep them solid.

"That's...good," she said, careful to keep her voice neutral. "The kids appreciate it, I'm sure."

He shrugged, eyes dipping. "It's nice, talking to them. Reminds me there's more to life than just my own issues."

The hush between them thickened. Jada's mind raced with everything unsaid. Part of her wanted to ask why he was suddenly so eager to be part of this community. Another part feared the answer.

Instead, she inhaled. "Look, Hakeem, I—" She hesitated. "I don't want to...jump to conclusions about your intentions. But the volunteering, the events... If it's just to impress me, you can stop."

His gaze snapped up, surprise flickering. "Jada, it's not—I mean, yes, I hope you notice, but it's also something I've been thinking about since I got here. I needed to do something meaningful besides just rehab. And Sweetgum...this is home, too."

She pressed her lips together. "You never called it home before."

He winced. "I know. I was a fool. I..." He cut himself off, dropping his voice lower. "I screwed up a lot of things, Jada. And I'm not expecting you to fix that for me. I just...want to be here. Genuinely."

A wave of conflicting emotions rose in her. *Trust isn't built overnight.* She reminded herself again of that fact, but the sincerity in his voice tugged at her walls. "Well," she said softly, "then…keep doing what you're doing. The kids could use some hope, especially if it comes from someone who's walked this path."

A flicker of relief passed over his face. "I will. And thank you for not telling me to back off."

Jada studied his brace, noticing he shifted his weight carefully as if mindful of overworking his knee. "Take care of yourself, too. Remember to ice that knee tonight."

A small smile touched his lips. "Yes, Doc."

Suddenly, she felt the urge to escape, aware of how easily she could get drawn into his warmth. She nodded briskly. "I need to go update patient notes. See you at your next session."

Without waiting for his response, she turned on her heel and headed down the corridor. Her footsteps echoed off the polished floor, each step carrying a swirl of uneasy hope. She couldn't deny how his actions—volunteering with kids, showing genuine interest in helping—chiseled away at her anger, bit by bit.

But anger wasn't the only thing in play. Hurt, fear, and the lingering question of whether this change in him was permanent all jostled in her chest. She'd have to watch carefully. And maybe, if he kept proving his intentions weren't just a show…

Maybe, she admitted in a whisper as she reached her office door, *there's room to believe in him again.*

CHAPTER TWELVE

It was a rare day off for Jada, a lull between rotating shifts at the hospital. She could have spent it catching up on laundry or streaming mindless TV, but restlessness pushed her out the door instead. Before she could question her decision, she found herself steering down the winding gravel road toward the Brown family's dairy farm.

She'd made vague plans with Rashad's wife, India, to drop by for some fresh produce—nothing too formal. It wasn't unusual for old friends to visit the farm, chat about life, and leave with a carton of eggs or a jug of fresh milk. But as she neared the long stretch of pasture, her stomach fluttered. What if *he* was here?

It's his family's farm; of course he might be around, she reminded herself. Still, she wasn't sure if she wanted to see him outside of therapy—and yet, part of her realized she was already bracing for it.

She parked near a row of tractors and slid out of the car. The late-morning sun bathed the fields in warm light, highlighting the gentle slope of rolling meadows dotted with cows. A faint breeze carried the scent of hay and earth. Jada drew a calming breath, stepping toward the big red barn where she spotted India waving enthusiastically.

"Hey, stranger!" India called, a broad grin lighting her features. She rested a hand on her baby bump—something Jada hadn't seen the last time they crossed paths. "It's good to see you. Thought you were never gonna come out this way."

Jada approached, returning the smile. "I've been meaning to visit. Work's been busy." She let her gaze flick to India's belly. "How are you feeling?"

India laughed softly. "Huge, sore, but happy. Rashad's been doting on me. He's around here somewhere."

Jada chuckled, nodding. "I wanted to pick up some fresh milk and eggs, if you have any spare. I'm thinking of trying a new healthy dessert recipe."

"We gotcha covered." India gestured toward a small side building where the farm kept recently packaged goods. "There's a fridge in there—help yourself. Pay in the jar if no one's around. Old-fashioned honor system."

They walked together, exchanging bits of small talk. India mentioned the upcoming local harvest event and teased that Jada should set up a booth for nutritional PT-friendly recipes. Jada laughed it off, though the idea planted a seed in her mind.

As they neared the door, a familiar voice drifted around the corner: "Rashad, I'll grab the feed bags. You get the gate."

Jada froze. *Hakeem.* Her pulse skipped.

Within seconds, Hakeem rounded the side of the barn, balancing a hefty sack of feed on his good shoulder. His knee brace was visible under his rolled-up jeans, but he moved more smoothly than she'd seen before—less of the tentative limp. He hadn't spotted Jada yet, focusing on maneuvering the bulky weight.

India glanced between them, a knowing flicker crossing her eyes. "I'll, uh, check the fridge," she murmured, slipping away discreetly.

Jada couldn't help but notice how Hakeem's arms flexed with the feed bag, his expression set in determined concentration. Then he looked up—and his eyes went wide, surprise flickering across his face.

"Jada," he said, the feed bag sagging a notch in his grasp. "I—hey."

Her throat felt dry. "Hi." Her gaze dipped to the heavy sack. "You sure you should be lifting that much with your knee?"

He shifted his weight, carefully setting the feed down. "It's part of my therapy, actually—gradual strength training. I'm going slow, but trying to rebuild."

She nodded, forcibly reminding herself that she wasn't on the clock here. "Well, be careful. You overdo it, and we'll have to backtrack."

He straightened, swiping sweat from his brow with the back of his hand. "Yes, Doc," he teased softly, though his voice held genuine respect.

She fought the urge to smile at his playful tone and instead folded her arms, glancing around. "You've been...busy. Volunteering at the hospital, working on the farm?"

"Yeah," he said, letting out a careful exhale. "Rashad's letting me help where I can, as long as I don't strain my knee. It's...nice to be part of the daily routine again. I used to hate the farm, remember?"

"I do," she said, recalling his teenage gripes about early mornings and farm chores. "Seems like you've changed your mind."

Hakeem gave a small shrug. "Guess I realized how much I missed it. Or maybe how much I took it for granted. It's honest work. Feels good to contribute."

An awkward pause settled, the summer air warm around them. Jada rubbed her palm against her arm, uncertain of how to navigate this casual encounter. It struck her that she hadn't been alone with him outside a therapy session since—*since everything.*

"I, um, came to pick up some eggs," she offered, trying to fill the silence with something ordinary.

He stepped aside, nodding toward the smaller building. "They're inside that cooler, labeled. Want me to help?"

"No, I've got it," she said quickly. Then she hesitated, meeting his gaze. "But thanks."

He nodded, expression gentle. "Sure."

They moved side by side toward the building, neither speaking. The moment felt strangely fragile—like if she looked too closely, her carefully maintained barriers would crack. She pressed her lips together, reminding herself that trust was a step-by-step process.

Inside, the small refrigeration room was cool and softly lit by a single overhead bulb. Rows of neatly stacked cartons lined shelves. Jada selected a carton of eggs, then a small jug of fresh milk. She deposited money in the tin jar, exactly as India had instructed.

Behind her, Hakeem lingered at the threshold. He seemed content to stand quietly, letting her take what she needed without hovering. That space, that respect, tugged at something inside her—a delicate thread of gratitude.

When she turned, he was studying her carefully. "You like to cook, huh?" he asked, voice light, bridging the space without pushing.

She swallowed. "Yeah. I started picking up healthy recipes during school. Turned into a hobby."

"That's cool," he said softly. "I remember you always trying to sneak vegetables into my meals."

A faint smirk crossed her lips at the memory of slipping spinach into his sandwiches. "You were always so dramatic about it."

They both let out a quiet laugh, the shared recollection

easing some of the tension. It felt good—almost too good—to fall back into that easy banter, if only for a second.

Jada cleared her throat. "I should probably get going," she said, hugging the carton to her chest like a shield. "Need to get these home before they spoil."

A hint of disappointment shadowed his features, but he nodded understandingly. "Yeah, sure." He stepped aside to let her pass, the door creaking as they emerged into the sunlight.

India was chatting with Rashad near the barn, and both seemed to notice Hakeem and Jada's exit but politely kept their distance. Hakeem walked her to the car, a gentle summer breeze rustling the tree line behind them.

She loaded her items into the trunk and closed it. For a moment, they stood near the driver's side door, neither quite knowing what to say. Finally, Jada inhaled.

"Thanks for…letting me get what I needed." *That sounded lame.* She pressed her lips together, trying again. "And, um, glad to see your knee's improving."

"It is," he said softly, eyes warm. "Thanks to you, really."

She shrugged, though her heart fluttered at the sincerity in his gaze. "That's my job."

"I know," he replied. His voice dropped just a fraction. "But you…you do it well. I appreciate it."

Heat prickled her cheeks. "All right, well, take care, Hakeem."

She slid into the driver's seat, shutting the door behind her with a firm click. Even through the glass, she saw him give a small wave as she started the engine. Her chest felt tight—conflicted between relief that they'd had a decent, civil exchange, and the painful awareness of how much had changed between them.

As she pulled away, Jada glanced in the rearview mirror. Hakeem stood in the farm's gravel driveway, arms crossed, the Georgia sun catching the lines of his strong shoulders. A stray pang of wistfulness hit her. Once upon a time, they might have spent a lazy afternoon together at the farm, laughing at chores, stealing quiet kisses.

Now it was all tentative steps and unspoken words. *Maybe that's okay,* she thought, forcing her grip to relax on the wheel. *At least we're moving forward—no matter how slowly.*

The farm receded in the distance behind her, but a new flicker of hope glowed in her chest. She couldn't predict the future, but for once, she didn't feel crushed by the past.

CHAPTER THIRTEEN

The bell over the diner door jingled as Hakeem stepped inside. He hadn't planned on stopping by Rochelle's tonight, but the thought of microwaved leftovers in his apartment hadn't exactly been motivating. At least here, there was noise—voices, clinking silverware, the hum of a place alive.

He slid onto a stool at the counter, nodding at Aimee when she appeared with a smile.

"Sweet tea?" she asked.

"You read my mind," he said, managing a grin.

As she walked away, a voice rang out from across the room. "Well, I'll be damned. Hakeem Brown in the flesh."

Hakeem turned, blinking in surprise as a tall, broad-shouldered man approached from a corner booth. His face was older, lined with a few years of hard work, but the grin was the same one Hakeem remembered from the locker room.

"Marcus Green," Hakeem said, standing to clasp his hand. "Man, it's been what—seven, eight years?"

"More like nine." Marcus chuckled, shaking his head. "Last time I saw you, we were celebrating that regional championship. You went off to chase the NFL, and I went off to chase…well, not much."

"You stayed around here?"

Marcus nodded, sliding into the stool beside him. "Yeah. Got married right out of high school, two kids now. Work construction most days. I help Coach Jones part-time with the JV squad when the season rolls around. Keeps me close to the game, you know?"

Aimee returned with Hakeem's tea and shot Marcus a curious smile before heading off again. Hakeem studied his old teammate, a strange mix of nostalgia and guilt tugging at him. Back then, he hadn't thought much about what happened to the guys who didn't get scholarships, who didn't leave town. He'd been too focused on escape.

"JV coaching," Hakeem said slowly. "That's solid. Bet those kids love having you around."

Marcus shrugged, but there was pride in his eyes. "It's something. They need role models. Keeps me honest, too." His gaze shifted, sharper now. "So what about you? Word is your knee is giving you trouble."

Hakeem stiffened, instinctively tugging at the brace under his jeans. "Yeah. Surgery, rehab. Trying to get back, but the docs don't sound too hopeful."

Marcus nodded like he understood. "That's rough, man. But football doesn't have to be over. You'd be good with the kids, too. You always saw the game better than anybody."

The suggestion landed heavier than Hakeem expected. Him, coaching? He'd never let his mind go there—not when he was still fighting to hang onto his pro career. But the thought lingered as Marcus grinned and clapped him on the back.

"Anyway, welcome home," Marcus said. "Don't be a stranger. We got a team cookout next week—Coach Jones likes to get the old players together before the season starts. You should come."

"I'll think about it," Hakeem replied, though part of him already knew he would.

Marcus excused himself to settle his bill, leaving Hakeem staring into his sweet tea, the ice clinking softly. Coaching. Community. Roots. He'd spent his whole life believing he had to leave Sweetgum behind in order to matter. But maybe the place was offering him another kind of future—one he hadn't been brave enough to imagine before.

CHAPTER FOURTEEN

*J*ada glanced at the clock on the therapy room wall. Hakeem was due any minute for his next appointment—an extended session focusing on building knee stability. She straightened the rolled towels and set out a foam roller, mentally ticking off her plan. These sessions had grown more comfortable yet still held that undercurrent of tension, like she was bracing for the past to strike without warning.

A soft rap at the door made her spine stiffen. "Come in," she called, putting on her professional mask.

Hakeem stepped inside, moving with more confidence than before. His brace was still visible under athletic shorts, but his gait was smoother. He offered a tentative smile. "Hey."

"Morning," Jada said with calm poise. She pointed to the exam table. "Let's start with your knee alignment checks. You can hop up there."

He obeyed, exhaling as he settled. She approached, placing warm hands gently around his knee. She felt for any lingering swelling or hot spots. The memory of touching him at that final session in high school—when everything was hopeful—flashed uninvited in her mind. She pushed it away.

"How's the farm work treating you?" she asked, keeping it casual as she rotated his leg gently.

A corner of his mouth quirked. "Not bad. Rashad's strict about me taking breaks, though. Won't let me lift more than I should."

She nodded. "Good. That means you're listening to your body, not rushing."

Their eyes caught briefly, something soft passing between them. She broke away, scribbling a note on her clipboard. "Range of motion looks good. We'll add slight resistance to your exercises today. Think you can handle it?"

He shifted, rolling his shoulder. "Yeah. Let's do it."

She moved to fetch a resistance band from the cupboard. "We'll keep reps low at first. Stay mindful—no sudden jerks."

Hakeem accepted the band from her, slipping it around his ankles. They worked through a series of precise, controlled motions. Every so often, she corrected his form with a gentle hand on his calf or thigh. She tried not to notice how her pulse quickened at the contact.

"Doing okay?" she asked, her professional tone tinged with the faintest concern.

He nodded, brow furrowed in focus. "Yeah. It's…challenging, but not impossible."

She offered an approving hum. "Good."

As they progressed, sweat beaded on his forehead. She sensed his determination to impress her—or maybe just to prove to himself that he wasn't defeated. When the final rep ended, she gave him a towel, noticing the strain in his eyes and the flush on his cheeks.

"Nice work," she said quietly. "You've come a long way from that first session."

He caught his breath. "Feels like it. Hard to believe it's only been a few weeks."

She dabbed some antiseptic gel on a cloth, wiping his knee brace gently. An unmistakable tension pulsed between them—the memory of how they used to clean up after high school workouts, giggling over sweaty towels and water bottles. But she kept her expression neutral.

He opened his mouth as if to say something more personal, then paused, reconsidering. Instead, he asked, "So...what's next?"

Jada breathed in, steeling herself. "We'll continue ramping up. That means a mix of balance drills, mild weight training, and eventually more challenging functional movements. If we keep going at this rate, you'll be able to jog again before long."

Hope glimmered in his eyes. "Jogging sounds like heaven compared to where I was."

She nodded, stepping away. "Just remember, you'll need consistent follow-through. I can't do the work for you."

Something wistful crossed his face. "Right. But...thank you, Jada... For everything."

She set down the cloth, heart twisting. "It's my job," she repeated, falling back on that well-worn mantra.

His gaze held hers. "I know it's more than that."

Her chest tightened. She swallowed and forced a brisk nod toward the door. "Head out to the hall for a cool-down walk, and I'll meet you at the front desk with your updated regimen."

Hakeem held her eyes for a second longer, then obliged. After he left, the room felt too quiet, the air tinged with the charge of unresolved emotions. Jada sank against the table, pressing a hand to her forehead. His sincerity, his gentle flirting around the edges of conversation—little by little, it was wearing on her.

She'd vowed to guard her heart. But the more she saw him genuinely commit to healing—and not just physically—the more she questioned if maybe he deserved a second chance at her trust.

~

FIVE MINUTES LATER, she found him near the reception desk, chatting with an older patient who recognized him from the NFL. His posture was relaxed, friendly—like he belonged here. And that notion both comforted and unnerved her.

She approached with the updated therapy plan, clearing her throat politely. "Here you go, Mr. Brown."

He accepted the sheet, scanning it. "Thanks, Dr. Davis."

The older patient, Ms. Turner, cocked a curious eyebrow at the polite formality. But Jada merely gave the woman a small smile. "Need anything else, Ms. Turner?"

"I'm good, dear," Ms. Turner said with a playful sparkle in her eye. She glanced between Jada and Hakeem, an amused smile tugging at her lips. "Enjoy your day, you two."

Jada felt her cheeks warm. She discreetly turned back to Hakeem. "So…that's it for today. Keep icing if there's any soreness. We'll meet again next week."

"Got it," he murmured, tucking the paper into his pocket. His eyes flicked toward the hospital entrance, where a few staffers were rearranging a bulletin board. "You heading back to your office?"

She hesitated, not wanting to linger in this charged moment. "Yes. I have more notes to log."

He nodded, stepping aside. "All right. See you next time."

She pivoted to leave, but a surge of daring made her pause. *Show him I'm not completely closed off.* She turned, catching him before he walked away. "Hakeem?"

He blinked, turning back. "Yeah?"

She swallowed. "You're making good progress. Keep it up."

The flash of gratitude in his smile warmed the air between

them. "Thanks," he said simply, as if that word held more than just appreciation. "I will."

With that, he exited the hospital, leaving Jada standing by the desk, heart drumming. It was a small moment, a tiny exchange. But it felt significant, like a crack in the armor she'd built. Maybe the day was inching closer when they could step beyond the wounds of the past—if they both dared to try.

She exhaled, heading for her office. *One step at a time,* she told herself. Because trust didn't blossom overnight, but each little gesture was a seed of possibility.

CHAPTER FIFTEEN

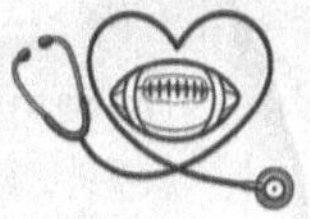

*J*ada Davis pressed her lips together, trying not to show her exasperation as she scanned the sign-up sheet taped to the community center's bulletin board. An impromptu *Sports Safety Workshop* had been scheduled at the last minute, and the hospital urged her—practically *begged* her—to lead a session on injury prevention for local teens.

She had no problem helping the community. In fact, she loved educating people on how to train and take care of their bodies. But she'd just learned that her "co-presenter" this evening was Hakeem Brown. Worse, the notice came from a hastily sent text by Anne, the hospital coordinator:

> Change of plans! Hakeem is volunteering to speak about his rehab journey. Sorry for late notice—you two will do great! 😊

Jada forced her breathing to remain calm. She could handle an accidental team-up. She'd do it for the kids. *Still*, being side by side with Hakeem, even in a professional setting, was a recipe for tension.

She strode into the small gymnasium section of the center, where a row of folding chairs faced a makeshift stage—a simple riser, a microphone, and a banner reading: *Keep Our Athletes Safe!*

A cluster of teenagers wandered around sporting team jackets or casual workout gear. They chatted excitedly about meeting the "NFL guy," a phrase that caused Jada's stomach to dip. *Of course, they'd be star-struck by him.*

She was setting pamphlets on a table when she felt a presence behind her. Turning, she nearly bumped into Hakeem. He wore a neat polo and comfortable athletic pants, knee brace barely visible beneath the fabric.

"Hey," he said quietly. "I just found out, too."

Jada lifted her chin. "Yeah," she replied, trying to keep any strain out of her voice. "I thought you'd be…somewhere else tonight."

He offered a small smile that didn't quite erase the worry in his eyes. "Anne roped me into sharing my experience. Guess we're sharing the spotlight."

She swallowed, turning back to the pamphlets. "Well, let's just get through this."

A flicker of resignation passed across his face, but he nodded. Before they could say more, a small group of kids jogged over. One boy, wearing a Sweetgum High letterman jacket, gaped at Hakeem like he was in the presence of a legend.

"Yo, you're *Hakeem Brown*! My pops said you and Dr. Davis here used to be, like, the biggest deal in our school's history—on and off the field!" His grin was wide with mischief.

Jada felt a prickle of alarm. *Here we go.*

Another teen chimed in, eyes dancing. "My auntie said y'all were the greatest love story Sweetgum High ever had—like prom king and queen times a thousand."

Snickers rose from the group. One of the girls teased, "You

gonna give us a talk about relationships, too, or just sports safety? 'Cause it sounds like y'all had it *all* for a minute."

Jada tensed, gripping the stack of pamphlets as the kids cackled, feeding off each other's energy. She shot Hakeem a wary glance, wishing she could vanish behind the table. But Hakeem raised his hands in mock surrender, a gentle humor sparking in his expression.

"Whoa, hold on," he said, addressing the teens calmly. "I'm here to talk about how you can protect your knees, ankles, and everything else so you can actually play your sport. But…" He paused, gaze sliding toward Jada for a moment. "…there is something to be learned about real life, too."

The kids leaned in, curious. One boy, looking about fifteen, folded his arms. "Yeah, well, my mom said if you'd stayed together, you'd have been the town's power couple. What happened?"

A ripple of laughter passed through the group, but behind it was genuine intrigue. Jada's pulse hammered.

Hakeem took a measured breath. He glanced at Jada as if asking permission to go on. Her heart thudded, but she gave a subtle nod, letting him choose his words.

He turned back to the teens, voice low but steady. "I messed up, plain and simple. I was so focused on my future—on playing ball—that I took for granted the people who supported me. Especially Dr. Davis. I figured that if we went our separate ways, we'd both be better off. But I realized too late how important she was to me—not just as a girlfriend, but as someone who truly had my back."

The teens went silent, suddenly captivated by this real-life drama. One girl let out a soft "Aw, man," and another elbowed her friend, eyes wide at the honesty. Jada's throat tightened.

Hakeem continued gently, "Thing is, no matter how good you are at your sport, or how far you go, if you don't take care of your relationships—the people who believe in you—you'll find yourself feeling empty. The trophies might shine, but they don't keep you company when you're lonely."

Some of the kids nodded thoughtfully. A tall, lanky boy in basketball shorts piped up, "So you're saying… don't ditch your folks just 'cause you got big plans?"

Hakeem nodded with a trace of regret. "Exactly. Don't lose sight of what's important. Life can change fast. One injury, one bad decision, and all the glory might be gone. But if you've kept your relationships strong, you'll still have a foundation."

The group murmured in awe, a couple teens turning to Jada with curious stares. She cleared her throat, pressing her palms together. "And from my perspective, if you plan to train at a high level, you can't ignore the people who keep you grounded. My job is to help athletes recover, but it's also about making sure their support system is solid—friends, family, coaches, partners. That support can make or break your comeback."

The kids soaked it in, some nodding, others teasing each other in hushed voices. One girl smirked, "So…y'all gonna get back together or what?"

Jada nearly dropped the pamphlets. A ripple of laughter spread through the group, and even a few parents standing nearby chuckled, eavesdropping on the lively exchange.

Hakeem glanced at Jada, warm regret and faint hope mingling in his gaze. "We're still…figuring things out," he said carefully. "But let's focus on you. Right now, your job is to respect your body and your relationships. That's how you win in the long run."

The teens exchanged grins and fist bumps, apparently satisfied with that answer. Jada offered a brisk nod, stepping forward to tap the workshop's pamphlet. "Anyway, these hand-outs have exercises for you to do at home—safe squats, lunges, core work—to protect your knees and ankles. Stick to them, and you'll have a better shot at staying healthy."

The organizer called the group to gather for the formal

presentation, pulling them away. They left behind a wave of giggles and side-glances, leaving Jada and Hakeem standing together in the aftermath.

She let out a careful breath, voice low. "Well, that was… unexpected."

He gave a small, rueful chuckle, eyes still reflecting the weight of what he'd just confessed. "Sorry if it put you on the spot."

She shook her head, the swirl of emotions settling into something complicated but not entirely unpleasant. "It's fine. At least they learned something…about sports *and* life, I guess."

His lips curved with gentle humor. "Guess so."

Before they could dwell on the tension, the workshop's organizer ushered everyone to their seats, calling for attention. Jada stepped forward, pressing forward into the official session —a safer zone of warm-ups, safety drills, and Q&A. As she and Hakeem took the makeshift stage, she felt her heart thudding at his admission. The teens had inadvertently forced him to lay out his regrets plainly for all to hear.

Surprisingly, it gave her a small ripple of solace—like a piece of the closure she'd never fully received. And from the way he handled the teens' questions, she saw glimpses of the thoughtful man behind the star athlete façade, the man she'd once trusted.

They worked through the presentation, showing the kids proper form for squats and lunges. Jada focused on mechanics while Hakeem discussed personal cautionary tales. The synergy flowed easily, almost like they were two halves of the same lesson plan.

When the session ended, parents and teens applauded. Many stuck around for one-on-one questions, snapping photos with Hakeem or asking Jada about advanced rehab techniques. Bit by bit, the crowd trickled out, leaving only a few stragglers to gather flyers.

Jada collected the leftover materials, her mind still whirling from the teens' blunt questions and Hakeem's raw honesty. As if summoned by her thoughts, he approached, hands in his pockets.

"That was something, huh?" he said, tone quiet.

She gave a short nod. "You handled it well. I didn't expect them to ask about us so directly."

He exhaled, shoulders easing. "Me neither. But maybe it's good they hear the truth—life's not just highlight reels and hometown fairy tales."

She studied him for a long moment, memories of their shared past flickering. "Yeah," she agreed softly. "It's not."

They stood there, the gymnasium almost empty, the air tinged with the residue of laughter and earnest curiosity. This forced proximity had laid bare some real truths—ones Jada wasn't sure how to process yet.

Still, a small piece of her tension had lifted. She reached for a box of supplies, and he grabbed the other side instinctively. They moved together, walking it to a nearby storage cart. With each step, Jada realized that despite the pain between them, they could still work in tandem.

When they set the box down, their eyes met in a moment of unspoken understanding. He gave her a gentle nod, a silent acknowledgment of the boundary they were treading. She nodded back, acknowledging that, at least for tonight, they were on the same page.

"See you, Jada," he said softly.

She tucked a stray lock of hair behind her ear, turning away. "See you," she murmured. And somehow, the regret in his voice didn't sting as fiercely as before.

CHAPTER SIXTEEN

*T*hree days after the impromptu workshop at the community center, Jada found herself at Sweetgum Park on a brisk late-afternoon. She'd volunteered—albeit reluctantly—to help out with a mini sports clinic for middle schoolers. Initially, the plan was just to demonstrate safe exercises, but word got around that Hakeem might be free to join.

"We need all the help we can get," the event organizer had said, beaming through the phone. "If you and Hakeem can both make it, the kids will get so much more out of it!"

Jada hadn't confirmed that Hakeem would show up—she had no idea. But she suspected fate, or small-town rumor, would place them side by side again. She sighed, gazing at the soccer field across from the pavilion. A gaggle of middle school athletes bounded around, giggling and tripping over untied shoelaces. All kids from the local rec leagues, bright-eyed and energetic.

Probably best if I come prepared, she thought, hugging her clipboard. She had a handful of basic warm-ups and cooldowns to walk them through, but truth be told, her nerves twisted at the notion of another forced proximity moment with Hakeem. The last workshop had ended with unexpected confessions from him—about how he'd messed up back in high school and what he'd lost. Part of her still reeled from hearing those words out in the open.

"Hey, Dr. Davis!" called a cheerful voice.

Turning, she saw a pair of the kids from the previous workshop trotting up. One wore a soccer jersey; the other clutched a basketball. They beamed at her.

"Are you gonna show us some new stretches?" the soccer player asked. "Last time, we used your pamphlet. Our coach said it helped."

Jada mustered a smile. "Glad to hear it. We'll do a quick session in a few. Let me set up, okay?"

They nodded, jogging off. In the distance, a group of parents lounged under the shade of tall sweetgum trees. Jada's attention drifted there, her heart doing a small flip when she spotted Hakeem talking to a couple of dads, all of them wearing casual athletic attire. He seemed relaxed, hands tucked in his pockets, nodding as they spoke.

She took a steadying breath. *Of course he's here.*

Cradling the clipboard, she strode over to a small table stacked with cones, balls, and water bottles. She was busy sorting them out when a low voice came from behind.

"Need a hand?"

She turned. Hakeem stood with an easy stance, knee brace partly visible under flexible pants. There was that flicker of tension again, overshadowed by a warmth in his eyes.

She cleared her throat. "Sure. You can set out the cones for the agility drills."

He nodded, stepping forward to help. As they gathered the neon cones, the air felt thick with unspoken thoughts. But Jada appreciated his quiet approach—no prying questions, no attempts to rehash the emotional confessions from before. They simply worked in tandem, placing the cones in neat rows across a patch of flat grass.

After a few minutes, a cheerful whistle cut through the air. The event organizer, Mr. Willis, stepped forward, calling the middle schoolers together. "All right, gather up! We're about to start!"

The kids scampered over, forming a haphazard semicircle around Jada and Hakeem. The two of them exchanged a quick look—an unspoken *we've got this*—before stepping up to address the group.

Jada raised her voice. "Welcome, everyone. I'm Dr. Davis, and this is—"

"Hakeem Brown!" a kid shouted, earning giggles from the rest.

She pressed her lips into a mild smile. "Yes. We're here to show you some safe ways to train, whether you play soccer, basketball, or anything else."

For the next twenty minutes, Jada took the lead, guiding them through basic dynamic stretches—lunges, leg swings, hip openers —occasionally demonstrating proper posture. Hakeem chimed in with real-life anecdotes: "Don't lock your knee on that squat— learned that one the hard way," which drew laughter from the kids.

When they shifted to cone drills, Hakeem took center stage, carefully explaining how to maneuver while keeping knees stable. Jada watched the kids line up and attempt zig-zag runs, giggling whenever they stumbled. Occasionally, Hakeem would lightly jog alongside them, encouraging them to keep form, though he was cautious with his own brace.

It all felt surprisingly…comfortable. Like old partners who'd found a new rhythm. She admired how patient he was, especially with the shy kids who hung back, uncertain. He coaxed them out with gentle humor, bridging the gap between star athlete and local mentor.

Eventually, the group took a water break, dispersing across the lawn. Jada and Hakeem found themselves momentarily alone near the table of supplies.

He wiped his brow with the back of his hand. "You think this is enough activity for them, or do we do a cooldown?"

She scanned the hot afternoon sun, noticing a few red faces among the kids. "Let's call them in for a cooldown. Don't want anyone to overheat."

Hakeem nodded. As they turned to gather the kids again, a tall girl approached, probably thirteen or fourteen, pushing braids from her eyes. She had a determined look about her.

"Mr. Brown? Dr. Davis?" She spoke softly, glancing between them. "I'm Jordan. My uncle told me y'all used to be the Sweetgum High 'it couple'—like, you were unstoppable. Is it true? For real, for real?"

A gentle laugh escaped Jada before she could stop it. *These rumors...* But she schooled her features. "We, uh, were close back then."

Hakeem's eyes flicked to Jada, a hint of that same regretful fondness from the workshop. He nodded. "Yeah, we did big things together...on and off the field."

Jordan twisted her fingers, looking anxious. "I'm just... scared. I love soccer, but there's so much pressure to practice every day, even when I'm sore. And my best friend said if I don't push harder, I'll never get a college scholarship. But..." She hesitated, gaze dropping. "What if I get hurt and lose everything? My parents can't afford big hospital bills."

Jada's heart tugged. She recognized that fear—putting dreams on the line, not sure which path to choose. She set a hand gently on Jordan's shoulder. "It's important to train smart. Overworking is how injuries happen. You have to rest, cross-train, and communicate with your coaches if something hurts. That's how you protect your future, not by ignoring pain."

Jordan nodded slowly, but her worry lingered. Hakeem took

a step closer, voice lowering, empathizing. "I know it feels like you have to push until you drop. But trust me, if you snap something, you're out for months—or forever. Real success isn't about never stopping; it's about balancing effort and self-care."

The teen looked back and forth between them. "Was that what messed things up for y'all? You pushed too hard?"

Hakeem paused, a flicker of solemn reflection passing over his face. "I pushed everything too hard—football, my future, and I left the people who mattered behind. I regret it. If I could go back, I'd pay more attention to the folks who supported me and to my own health. Both are more fragile than you think."

Jordan stared, absorbing his honesty, then asked softly, "So… you think being with people you care about is as important as training every day?"

Jada felt a subtle swell in her chest at the teen's insight. Hakeem held the girl's gaze. "Absolutely," he said. "Having the right support system keeps you grounded. Don't push away your friends, family—or your own body's signals—just to chase a dream blindly. The dream won't mean much if you're hurting or alone."

A hush settled, as though Jordan realized she'd stumbled on something deeper. She offered a small, grateful smile. "Thanks. I… appreciate that."

She stepped away, presumably to rejoin the water break group, leaving Jada and Hakeem standing there with an odd sense of vulnerability hanging in the air. That question about them—*Was that what messed things up for y'all?*—echoed in Jada's mind. Maybe it was. Maybe it was a piece of it.

Hakeem exhaled, casting Jada a glance that teemed with unspoken apology. She straightened, blinking away the emotional weight, remembering they were here for the kids. "Come on," she said quietly. "Cooldown time."

They gathered the group once more, guiding them through gentle stretches. Jada demonstrated calf and quad stretches while Hakeem coached from the side, cautioning against bouncing movements that strain muscles. A quiet synergy again, despite the swirl in Jada's heart.

When they wrapped up, the kids chattered excitedly, a few coming up to show off how limber they felt. Parents lingered, snapping photos. A wave of satisfaction washed over Jada—she truly loved seeing them learn safer ways to train.

Finally, the event organizer thanked everyone, giving Jada and Hakeem a special shoutout. As the crowd dispersed, Jada started packing up the leftover pamphlets. She fully expected Hakeem to slip away, but he stepped over, kneeling carefully to fold the cones with her.

"Thanks for today," he murmured. "You led the session well."

She tucked some pamphlets into a bag. "We both did our part."

He glanced around, noticing the last of the families wandering off. "I never thought we'd be doing something like this, you know—teaching kids together."

She let out a soft, rueful hum. "Life's funny that way."

He looked like he wanted to say more, but then the breeze carried distant laughter from the kids. Jada gathered the final items, uncertain how to handle the sudden closeness.

"Hey—" he began, voice quiet. She turned, eyebrows lifted in question. "About that girl's question," he said. "I meant what I told her. I took for granted a lot back then... especially you."

She couldn't deny the sincerity in his tone. Her chest tightened. "Hakeem—"

He held up a hand, a gentle gesture to keep her from feeling cornered. "I'm not asking anything. Just wanted you to know I recognize where I went wrong."

A flicker of sadness and hope warred inside her. "Okay," she murmured, voice just loud enough for him to hear.

They stood in silence, the park growing quieter under the

late-afternoon sun. After a moment, Jada cleared her throat. "We should probably return this equipment."

"Yeah," he agreed softly, taking half the load from her arms. "Let's go."

They walked side by side toward the rec center storage shed, neither pressing the conversation further. Yet Jada couldn't stop replaying his words. She might not be ready to surrender her heart, but each day, he chipped away at the walls she'd built, showing a different side of himself—a man who knew what he'd lost and regretted it deeply.

As they tucked the sports gear away, Jada realized something surprising: maybe she didn't mind this forced proximity so much. Maybe, under the right circumstances, it gave them both a chance to remember what once made them such a strong team. And for the first time, that realization didn't sting—it felt almost hopeful.

She shut the shed door, the latch clicking into place. In the quiet that followed, Hakeem glanced her way with a gentle nod. "Thanks again."

She mustered a calm, steady look. "You, too. I'll see you around."

He hesitated like he might add something else, but ended up offering a small, warm smile instead. They parted, each walking to their cars. A sense of cautious optimism fluttered in Jada's chest. *One step at a time,* she reminded herself.

Because while old wounds ran deep, days like this reminded her that healing—even the emotional kind—could be possible if both parties were willing to keep trying.

CHAPTER SEVENTEEN

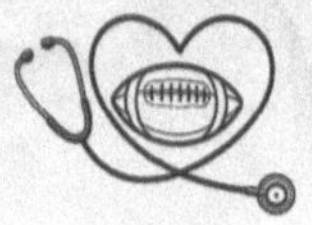

The 'team cookout' was much larger than Hakeem thought it would be. Seemed like the whole town showed up.

Smoke curled up from the grill pits at Sweetgum Meadows Community Park, lazy ribbons of hickory threading through the thick, late-summer air. Kids wove between picnic tables with neon cups of lemonade. Somebody's uncle argued good-naturedly over a game of spades. Old-school R&B thumped from a portable speaker near the pavilion, bass soft enough to let the cicadas keep their own steady rhythm.

Hakeem shifted his weight off his bad leg and tried not to look like he was guarding it. The brace was hidden under dark jeans, but his knee still had opinions about uneven grass. He balanced a paper plate in one hand and let the other hang loose, forcing himself to breathe like he belonged here—as if he hadn't spent years sprinting in the opposite direction.

"Thought I was gonna have to send a search party," Marcus said, appearing at his elbow with a grin and two bottled waters. "Coach swore you'd show."

"Smelled the food from down the street," Hakeem said, taking a bottle. "Figured I oughta investigate."

Marcus snorted. "You figured you might see Jada. I don't know who you're trying to fool."

Hakeem didn't bite. He kept his eyes on the grill line where Coach Jones—whistle still on, because some habits didn't retire—flipped beef ribs with the calm of a man who'd won and lost enough to know neither lasted forever. Malachi moved through the crowd with a tray of cornbread, sleeves rolled, passing pieces like communion.

"Brown!" Coach called when he finally looked up. "You gonna stand there posing or are you gonna eat?"

"Sir, yes sir," Hakeem answered, stepping into line because there was never any point arguing with Coach.

He collected ribs and beans and a wedge of cornbread, then slid down to make room for the next wave. He was halfway to the end of the buffet when a familiar scent—coconut and something warm—hit him before the voice did.

"Please tell me there's still cobbler left."

Jada.

She was two people behind him, curls gathered at the nape of her neck, a sleeveless sundress the color of ripe peaches hugging her in a way that made breathing a chore. She hadn't seen him yet; she was laughing at something Aliyah said, one hand tipping a paper plate to keep the collard greens from sliding off.

Hakeem's chest did that unhelpful tight thing it had been doing since the first day he'd walked back into her life and found her in a white coat with his chart in her hands. He didn't move—didn't want to spook either of them—but when the line shuffled forward, Aliyah glanced up and clocked him. Her brows lifted; then, to his surprise, she gave a small nod like, *Be cool.*

"Hey," Jada said a beat later, as if she'd felt the air change and followed it with her eyes. The smile she'd had for her friend settled into something quieter, careful but not cold. "Mr. Brown."

"Evening, Dr. Davis." He kept his tone light. "You off duty? Or you gonna chase me around the park telling me to ice?"

"Depends," she said, and for a second the corner of her mouth tipped. "Are you following your regimen?"

"Religiously," he lied. Then, because her eyebrow went up in the exact way that said *don't test me*, he amended, "Mostly."

Aliyah bumped Jada with her hip. "I'm taking this child to the dessert table before she lectures you in public," she said to Hakeem, all mischief. "Nice to see you, Hakeem." She tugged Jada forward, but not before adding with a mock-whisper, "Save your charming for later. I want peach cobbler before it's gone."

They drifted on with the line. Hakeem let out a breath he wouldn't have admitted he was holding and stepped out of the way to the edge of the pavilion, where folding tables had seen better paint jobs. He didn't sit. Eating standing up meant less pressure on the joint, and it gave him an excuse to keep his eyes moving—on Coach with the tongs, on Rashad laughing too loud near the coolers, on kids throwing a too-large football in a too-small space.

"Mr. Brown!" One of the kids had peeled off from the pack, hair in tight twists, eyes bright. "Is it true you could read a coverage before the snap? Marcus said."

Hakeem glanced toward Marcus, who lifted his soda like *my bad*.

"Sometimes," Hakeem said. "Mostly I was guessing pretty and praying it worked."

The kid grinned. "Can you show us how?"

Hakeem's knee pulsed a warning. He weighed it. Then he caught sight of Jada at the end of the dessert table, her hands busy, her attention not on him, and thought, *You wanted to show up. So show up.*

"Grab your crew," he said to the kid. "We'll do it right here. No hero moves, no diving."

They marked out makeshift yard lines with water bottles and one abandoned flip-flop. Hakeem took the spot where a center would be, the kids fanning out on a patch of trampled clover. He walked them through it—how to set your feet, how to use a quick shoulder glance to shift a defender, how to read the shallow safety if your gut said blitz.

"Eyes lie," he told them, tapping his temple. "Feet tell the truth. Trust the feet."

They ran it slow, then a hair faster. Hakeem didn't drop back more than a step, but muscle memory lit up like a string of bulbs anyway, the rhythm of the game whispering *see, you still know.* He tossed the ball on a short arc to the kid with the twists. It hit his hands clean. The circle exploded—cheers, chest bumps, a little too much swagger for a ten-yard gain.

"Again?" the kid asked, breathless.

"Two more," Hakeem said. "Then y'all give the park back before you take out Ms. Hattie's potato salad."

They ran two more. On the last throw, his knee pinched and he adjusted mid-motion, dropping his arm angle to flick the ball around a phantom rusher. It cost him; a hot wire zipped up his thigh to his hip. He masked the wince with a smile, clapped hands with the boys, and sent them sprinting toward the pavilion with a stern, "Walk near the food, unless you want Aimee to make you scrub dishes."

As the group broke, he caught Jada watching. She was leaning near the end of a table, a plastic fork caught in her fingers like she'd forgotten what to do with it. When their eyes met, she didn't look away. Something like pride flared there— gone as soon as it arrived, replaced with professional appraisal.

She crossed the grass to him, not so close that the town could call it anything, not so far that it could be mistaken for avoidance.

"That last step looked sharp," she said. "Sharp like 'I told you not to overdo it' sharp."

He huffed a laugh. "You saw that, huh?"

"I see a lot of things," she said, and for a heartbeat, it wasn't a warning. It was a memory.

Hakeem swallowed. The urge to fill the space with an apology rose hard and sudden. He tamped it down. Not here. Not like this.

"I'll ice when I get home," he said instead. "Promise."

"Fifteen on, fifteen off." She pointed toward the cooler like she had the right to boss him around—which, technically, she did. "And keep the brace snug tonight. Swelling looked mild at your last session, and I'd like to keep it that way."

"Yes, ma'am."

A toddler barreled by and clipped Jada's side; Hakeem's hand shot out on instinct, steadying her elbow. Her skin was warm. He let go immediately. She'd always balanced him without needing help. He wasn't sure which of them was recognizing that more loudly.

"Thank you," she murmured.

"No problem," he said. He worked a breath in and out. "Jada, I—"

"Hey! You two seen the cobbler?" Rashad boomed from behind them, a foil pan in each hand like trophies. "Aimee's about to put out a fresh one, but y'all better move fast. Ms. Hattie is on plate three and I'm not starting a family war."

Jada laughed, the sound lighter than the sky felt, and took a step back. "Duty calls. Don't test Ms. Hattie."

"Wouldn't dream of it," Hakeem said.

She hesitated. The crowd moved around them—friends, cousins, kids tugging sleeves. "You handled those boys well," she said softly. "They listen when you talk."

"I had a good coach," he said, tipping his chin toward the grill. Then, because honesty seemed like the only thing that didn't make a mess, he added, "And a good…person who told me to slow down when I didn't want to."

Jada's lashes lowered for a fraction, like the words had grazed a bruise. "See you Tuesday," she said, sliding the professionalism back into place. "Bring the exercise sheet. We're increasing resistance."

"Yes, Doc."

She turned, and the peach dress caught the light as she moved toward the dessert station, Aliyah materializing at her side like an anchor. Hakeem watched long enough to see Jada laugh at something her friend said, to see her accept a slice of cobbler and press the fork down through the top crust with a little hum that used to undo him.

"Man," Marcus said, reappearing with two cups of sweet tea, "if longing was visible you'd owe the town a privacy screen."

"Shut up," Hakeem said, but he was smiling, weak thing though it was.

Marcus handed him a cup. "You good?"

Hakeem took a sip and let the sugar sit on his tongue. He glanced at Jada across the way, then at Coach at the grill, at Rashad arguing sauce recipes with Ms. Hattie like he wasn't about to lose. He breathed again—deep this time, all the way to the ache.

"I'm here," he said, mostly to himself. "I'm showing up."

Marcus bumped his shoulder. "Then keep doing it. Small yards still move chains."

"Look at you, Mr. Wisdom."

"Don't get used to it."

They stood there a while longer, letting the evening settle. When the sun ducked behind the pines and string lights flickered on, Hakeem handed his empty cup to Marcus and limped toward the trash can, accepting the pinch as the price of the moment. He didn't make any speeches. Didn't chase her down. He let the night end the way it wanted to—ordinary, warm, the kind of memory you could carry without dropping anything.

On his way back past the grill, Coach lifted the tongs in salute. "Stop by practice tomorrow," he said. "The JV needs a lesson in feet telling the truth."

Hakeem nodded. "Yes, sir."

He looked once more toward the dessert table. Jada had cobbler in one hand and was waving a fork at Aliyah, arguing the merits of vanilla ice cream versus whipped cream like the answer might change the world. She caught him watching and didn't flinch. Didn't smile either. But her gaze lingered a heartbeat longer than polite.

Small yards, he thought, and felt something in his chest uncoil. He could live with that. He could build a life with that.

He turned toward the field and the boys and the work that waited, the smell of smoke and sugar chasing him all the way to the parking lot.

CHAPTER EIGHTEEN

Jada stepped inside the diner, relieved to find the usual lunchtime rush had mellowed into a cozy bustle. She slid into a booth near the window and glanced around. Familiar sights comforted her: the gleaming counter, the warm chatter, and the scent of soul food drifting from the kitchen.

She hadn't planned to come here. But after a busy morning at the hospital, she craved a comforting meal and a moment of quiet. Her thoughts still whirled with recent events—helping at the sports clinic, hearing Hakeem's heartfelt regrets, and feeling her own defenses slowly peel away. A new kind of uncertainty gripped her: *Am I truly ready to let him in again?*

Before she could delve further into her mental debate, a cheery voice broke through. "Dr. Davis!" called Aimee, beaming from behind the counter. She wore her usual apron, her hair pulled into a neat ponytail. "Grab a seat; I'll be right with you!"

Jada waved back. "No rush!"

While she waited, she spotted a couple of older women—pillars of the town—steeped in conversation at a nearby table. They were part of the ever-present circle of "aunties" who knew everyone's business. Jada recognized Mrs. Andrews and Mrs. Bridges, quietly sipping sweet tea, glancing in her direction with interest. She offered them a polite nod, bracing herself for potential gossip.

Sure enough, the two exchanged whispers, then approached her booth. Mrs. Andrews spoke first, her voice warm but curious. "Well, look who's here. Haven't seen you in a few days, dear."

"Work's kept me busy," Jada said, a friendly but guarded smile on her face.

Mrs. Bridges nudged Mrs. Andrews aside so she could lean in conspiratorially. "Busy, hmm? We hear you been crossing paths with that Brown boy again—forced to do these sports things together." She gave an exaggerated wink. "You know we're all rootin' for a *certain kind* of happy ending, sugar."

Jada stifled a cough, quickly shaking her head. "Let's not jump to conclusions. We're just...collaborating on community events. That's all."

Mrs. Andrews pressed a hand to her heart with theatrical disappointment. "Well, folks sure are talkin'. You two were the best thing since cornbread muffins back in the day."

Jada opened her mouth to respond, but a gentle laugh escaped Aimee as she arrived with a menu in hand. "Ladies, you're gonna scare off my customer. Give Dr. Davis some breathing room, now."

The aunties grinned unapologetically. Mrs. Bridges patted Jada's shoulder. "We'll let you eat in peace, darling. Just know we're cheerin' on *whatever* you do."

They ambled away, leaving Jada's face set in an exasperated but faintly amused expression. Aimee slid the menu across the table, eyes twinkling. "Small town, huh?"

"Small town," Jada echoed, flipping open the menu to buy herself a moment. She felt the weight of those aunties' words lingering. "I'll take the grilled chicken salad, please."

Aimee nodded, scribbling on her notepad. "Sure thing. And a sweet tea to go with it?"

"Perfect."

Once Aimee left, Jada settled against the booth, exhaling. She scanned her phone for a moment, checking messages from the hospital—nothing urgent. Despite the older women's meddling, she found her mind drifting back to the events with Hakeem: the quiet moments afterward, his genuine remorse, the care in his eyes when he warned kids against repeating his mistakes.

He's changed. The thought came unbidden. She remembered how brash he could be at 18, convinced the world revolved around football. Now, he was teaching others not to sacrifice everything for the game. He'd also been the first to show up at volunteer events, quietly supporting local kids. The transformation was hard to ignore.

She was so lost in reflection that she didn't notice the door chime. It wasn't until a familiar voice reached her ears that her stomach did a small flip.

"Hey, Aimee," Hakeem greeted from across the diner. "I'll just grab a seat anywhere?"

Aimee nodded, gesturing to the open booths. "Sure thing, honey. I'll be over in a sec."

Jada's heart thudded. *Speak of the devil.* She watched him glance around, clearly scanning for a table. Then his gaze locked on her. For an instant, they both froze.

He could have chosen a booth across the room. It would've been polite, maybe easier. Instead, after a brief hesitation, he limped carefully toward her, his posture tentative. She could practically see the question in his eyes: *Mind if I join?*

She offered the slightest nod, not quite trusting her voice. He slid into the opposite seat, setting his phone aside, knee brace peeking under his pant leg.

"Didn't know you'd be here," he said softly, sounding unsure if it was okay to speak.

She pulled in a steady breath. "Me neither. Just needed lunch."

He drummed his fingers on the table for a second before clasping them together. "I can go if you want—"

"No," Jada cut in gently. "You're fine. It's a public diner."

A flicker of relief crossed his face. The tension between them was palpable, but not entirely uncomfortable. More...charged with possibility.

Aimee returned, eyebrows lifted at the sight of them together. She handed Jada's sweet tea over, then turned to Hakeem. "You want the usual? Turkey sandwich and iced water?"

He nodded. "Yep, thanks."

Once Aimee stepped away, a hush settled over the booth. Jada sipped her tea, eyes wandering around the diner, searching for safe conversation topics. She spotted Mrs. Andrews and Mrs. Bridges across the room, grinning from ear to ear at the sight of them together. *Great.*

Finally, Hakeem spoke. "How's your day? Busy at the hospital?"

She relaxed a fraction. "Mostly routine follow-ups this morning. Nothing major."

He ran a hand over his knee brace. "Good. Less stress for you."

A half-smile formed on her lips. "It's always some level of stress."

They lapsed into silence again, but it felt slightly easier than before. She found herself studying him—how he seemed calmer, shoulders not so tense. The same man who once breezed through life with starry-eyed ambition now carried himself with a certain humility.

When Aimee placed their lunches on the table, Jada thanked her. She speared a forkful of her salad, noticing how Hakeem took a careful bite of his sandwich, avoiding sudden movements that might jar his knee. They ate quietly for a moment.

"Hey, Dr. Davis?" Jada glanced up to see a teenage boy approach shyly, wearing an older version of the Sweetgum High jersey. "We had that workshop at the community center, remember me?"

She recognized him—Tarik, a shy defensive back. "Sure, Tarik. How's your ankle?"

He lit up at being remembered. "It's way better, thanks to those ankle-strengthening exercises you showed me." Then his gaze flicked to Hakeem, and he broke into a sheepish grin. "Uh, Mr. Brown, you think you'll talk to the high school team sometime? They'd freak if you came by."

Hakeem exchanged a look with Jada, searching for her reaction before answering. She nodded subtly, giving him permission. So he turned to Tarik, smiling. "I can try to arrange that. Once the coach invites me, I'll do what I can."

Tarik fist-pumped the air. "Awesome! My guys are gonna lose it!" With that, he hurried off, likely to share the news.

Jada let out a small laugh when he was out of earshot. "Word travels fast. The kids look up to you, you know."

Hakeem's eyes glimmered with the faintest pride. "Yeah, I never expected to be a mentor type, but..." He shrugged. "It's nice."

"It suits you," she offered, surprising herself with the compliment. But it felt true.

He toyed with the edge of his sandwich. "Thanks."

At the corner of her vision, Jada noticed Mrs. Andrews and Mrs. Bridges leaning forward, all ears. She rolled her eyes inwardly. "We have an audience," she murmured to Hakeem, tilting her head slightly at the two older women.

He followed her gaze, exhaling a soft chuckle. "They've always been a nosy bunch."

"Still are," Jada teased back, voice low.

For a moment, it felt like a flash of the old days, exchanging secret jokes about the town busybodies. The warmth of it seeped into her chest, reminding her how much she'd missed this easy banter. But caution hovered in her mind, reminding her not to tumble blindly into nostalgia.

After they finished eating, they lingered, neither rushing to leave. Aimee cleared their plates with a knowing smile and left them to chat. Once more, Jada found herself on the brink of letting him in.

Eventually, he checked his watch. "I've got therapy exercises to do this afternoon. Gotta stay on track."

A flicker of professional pride touched her. "Good. Don't slack off, or we'll have to redo half your progress."

"Wouldn't dream of it," he said, voice earnest.

They stood, drifting toward the register. Jada expected him to reach for the bill, but he paused—clearly recalling how she insisted on splitting costs last time. She nodded, placing half the payment on the counter while he placed the other.

Mrs. Bridges sidled up, brandishing her to-go coffee like a microphone. "Well, I'll be! Y'all paying together? That's as close to a date as we've seen in a minute."

Hakeem held up a hand in mock surrender. "Now, Ms. Bridges—"

She grinned, then whispered loudly, "Just sayin', this town would love to see you two back in each other's good graces... if you catch my meaning."

Jada forced a light laugh. "We hear you, Ms. Bridges. Have a good day." She gently steered Hakeem toward the door, ignoring the older woman's conspiratorial wink.

Outside, the midday sun glowed across Main Street. Cars meandered by; a few people strolled in and out of shops. Hakeem hesitated on the sidewalk, turning to Jada with a tentative smile. "That was...nice."

She nodded. "Yeah. It was." No point denying it. For all the tension, their quick lunch had felt comfortable in a way that caught her off-guard.

"Thanks for not minding that I joined you," he said. "I know it's still…complicated."

"It is," she agreed softly. "But maybe it doesn't have to be hostile."

His gaze held the faintest glimmer of hope. "I'd like that—a chance to build something… friendlier, at least."

Jada inhaled the warm air, heart fluttering. "We'll see."

He accepted that with a small nod. "See you at therapy, Doc."

She let out a breath. "See you then, Mr. Brown."

And with that, they parted ways, each heading down Main Street in opposite directions. The watchers in the diner likely had a new chapter of gossip to mull over, but Jada didn't mind for once. Because for the first time since Hakeem's return, she felt less like they were dancing around a wound, and more like they were gently bandaging it—together.

CHAPTER NINETEEN

Jada gripped the steering wheel as she pulled into her parents' driveway, relieved to see her mom's car parked alongside her dad's old sedan. The small ranch-style house, painted a soft cream color, looked as warm and inviting as she remembered from childhood. A wave of nostalgia washed over her—the sound of cicadas in the tall oak trees, the neat flower beds her mom tended meticulously, the front porch where she used to sit and dream about a life beyond Sweetgum.

She stepped out, smoothing her shirt before heading up the short walkway. Truthfully, she wasn't sure if she had the emotional energy for a family dinner tonight—especially after all the ups and downs with Hakeem. But when her mother insisted *"We haven't seen you in too long!"*, Jada couldn't say no.

"Baby girl!" her mother called the moment Jada opened the front door. The tantalizing aroma of baked chicken and collard greens floated through the small foyer.

"Hey, Mom," Jada greeted, hugging her. "Something smells amazing."

Her mom—Veronica Davis—stepped back, hands planted on

her hips. "Been slaving over that stove for hours. Don't let it go to waste." She pointed playfully, then turned back toward the kitchen.

In the living room, Walter Davis, Jada's dad, lifted his head from the newspaper. He broke into a grin. "There's my daughter. How's the big-time hospital life?"

Jada shrugged, plopping onto the worn couch next to him. "You know, busy as always. But it's good."

Walter peered at her over his glasses. "Mm-hmm. You sure you're not overworking yourself? You look like you got a lot on your mind."

Before she could dodge, Veronica called from the kitchen, "Jada, grab some ice from the garage fridge for the tea!"

Jada popped up, grateful for the distraction. She slipped into the garage, rummaging for a bag of ice in the old upright freezer. Her dad followed moments later, leaning against the doorframe.

He folded his arms. "So, how's everything really going?"

She half-smiled, shaking some frost off the ice bag. "I'm okay, Dad. Just…managing."

His brow rose. "Managing, huh? That secret code for something your old man might need to know?"

She sighed, tugging on the freezer door to close it. "If you must know, Hakeem's back in town. We keep running into each other through volunteer stuff and at the hospital. It's… complicated."

Walter whistled softly. "Well, I'll be. Last I heard he was playing pro ball. And you two—"

"Dad, don't start," she warned, though her tone was more resigned than irritated. "You know how it ended."

He held up his hands in a peace gesture. "Just checking if it's still an open wound or if there's a chance for, you know, closure."

She frowned down at the ice bag. "I'm not sure yet. He's

changed. Or at least he seems different. And I can't decide how to feel about it."

Walter rested a reassuring hand on her shoulder. "Take it slow, baby girl. If he's serious, he'll show it with actions. Don't forget, you're not the same person you were at eighteen either."

She let out a long breath. "That's what I'm afraid of—we've both changed so much. Not sure if we fit together like we used to."

Her dad gave a gentle nod, then straightened. "Well, come on. Don't leave your mama's dinner getting cold. We'll talk more later if you want."

They returned to the kitchen, where Veronica fussed over the final touches of the meal. The dining table was set with mismatched plates, and the walls carried the same framed family photos that had been there since Jada was a kid. Moments later, they all settled in—Walter at one end, Veronica at the other, and Jada somewhere in between.

Conversation flowed easily at first: updates on extended family, tidbits about local events. But as soon as the plates were filled, her mother's gaze sharpened, zeroing in on Jada the way only a parent could.

"Word around town is that you and that Brown boy have been at a bunch of these community events—sports clinics, hospital visits. Not to mention folks saw you both in the diner."

Jada closed her eyes briefly. *The entire town is fixated on me and Hakeem, apparently.* She cleared her throat. "We've done volunteer stuff together. That's all."

Veronica arched an eyebrow. "That's all, huh? Because Mrs. Bridges—bless her gossipin' heart—said you two looked mighty comfortable."

Walter snorted, spooning a healthy serving of collard greens onto his plate. "Leave her be, Ronnie. They're grown folks. We can't force 'em to talk about it."

Veronica waved off Walter's protest. "I'm just saying, we

loved Hakeem once. You know that, right, Jada? He used to come around here all the time, always with that big grin, sneaking extra dessert when he thought I wasn't looking." She shook her head with a smirk. "I never knew what truly broke y'all apart—only that he left for football and you went off to college."

A stretch of silence fell, thick with old pain. Jada prodded her fork at a piece of chicken, recalling the ache of that final conversation under the high school stadium lights. "We were just kids," she said quietly. "He wanted to protect me from all the long-distance mess. I guess he assumed we'd grow apart anyway."

Walter set his fork down, eyes tender. "He might've thought he was doing right, but it hurt you bad."

She nodded slowly, feeling a tightness in her chest. "It did."

Veronica reached across the table, patting Jada's hand. "Well, if he's come back and seems sorry, maybe he deserves a chance to prove it."

Jada blinked in surprise, not expecting such direct encouragement. "Mom…"

Veronica's expression softened. "I'm not telling you to jump in arms wide open. Just…don't let old wounds keep you from seeing who he is now."

Jada swallowed, heat prickling at the back of her neck. "Yeah. I get that. I'm…trying."

Her parents exchanged knowing smiles. They moved on to safer topics—Walter's annoyance with the local cable company, Veronica's new routine at the local gym. All the while, Jada ate in contemplative silence, letting her mother's words marinate in her mind.

After dinner, Jada helped clear the table, rinsing dishes while her dad dried them. Once the kitchen was back in order, Walter caught her eye. "Why don't we sit on the porch for a bit?"

She nodded, stepping outside with him. The late-afternoon

sun cast a soft glow over the street, crickets starting their evening chorus. They settled onto the worn porch swing, the wood creaking softly beneath them.

"Listen," Walter began, gaze on the quiet road. "If you ever want to talk about him—about how you feel—I'm here. No pressure. I just remember how you were back then. You lit up whenever he came around."

She gazed at the cracked sidewalk, recalling late-night phone calls and stolen kisses with Hakeem when they were both too young to see beyond Friday night lights. "I was in love," she admitted quietly. "But that was a long time ago."

Walter's tone was gentle. "Feelings can change. But that doesn't mean you can't find something new. A different kind of love, you know? More mature, less naive."

Jada took a moment to absorb that. A breeze rustled the leaves overhead. "We'll see," she whispered. "He's…making an effort, Dad. But I'm scared."

He patted her back. "You've got a good head on your shoulders. No need to rush. Just keep your eyes open."

They fell into a comfortable silence, the creak of the swing underscoring the hush of the neighborhood. Jada breathed in the faint scent of jasmine from her mother's flower bed, feeling a sliver of peace. Maybe she didn't have all the answers, but at least she had a supportive family, a career she loved, and a spark of cautious hope for what might come next.

Eventually, the sun dipped lower, and Jada said her good-byes, promising to visit again soon. She stepped into her car, mind still replaying her parents' words. As she drove away, she realized a new sense of clarity glimmered in her chest.

She wasn't ready to forgive or forget everything, but she wasn't prepared to shut Hakeem out entirely, either. *Maybe that's a start,* she thought, turning onto the main road. *A small one, but a start, nonetheless.*

CHAPTER TWENTY

Hakeem adjusted the cuff of his button-down and stood for a moment outside the freshly painted Victorian that now housed the Sweetgum Meadows Bed and Breakfast. Lavender trim. Fresh shutters. He could admit it looked good, though a younger version of himself would've rolled his eyes at the fuss. Rochelle had vision—always had—and judging from the smell of cinnamon drifting from inside, she hadn't lost her touch.

He hadn't exactly signed up for a festival committee. Marcus had dragged him into it, saying it was about time he started "showing his face" at community events again. Maybe he was right. Either way, it felt strange standing on the porch of a B&B instead of a stadium tunnel, waiting to talk about pie contests and safety booths.

The screen door squeaked as he pushed it open. Warmth and pastry-scented air hit him, carrying the hum of voices deeper inside. Rochelle appeared from the hallway, all floral blouse and bigger-than-life energy.

"Well, if it ain't Sweetgum's own star!" she said, swooping in for a hug before he could brace himself. "Look at you, acting like you don't know how to come home."

Hakeem chuckled, returning the embrace. "Good to see you, Ms. Rochelle. Place looks great."

"Mm-hm. And don't you go buttering me up. Come on, Benjamin's got the parlor full of folks already."

He followed her down a narrow corridor and into a room that looked like it had leapt from a postcard: high ceilings, patterned wallpaper, Victorian chairs lined up in a semicircle. On the back table, coffee and a tray of scones perfumed the air. Familiar faces dotted the room—Ms. Zhang from the Chinese restaurant, Mr. Willis from rec league sports, a handful of others.

And then there was Jada.

She'd just stepped in behind Rochelle, tote sliding off her shoulder. For a second she froze, eyes catching his. That polite nod she gave him hit like a jab—acknowledgment without warmth—but he forced a small smile and dipped his head back. His shoulders tightened all the same.

He took a seat near Benjamin, grateful when the older man launched straight into agenda talk. Rochelle clapped her hands, corralling attention. "All right, people. Harvest Festival's coming quick, and we got work to do."

Discussion spun through logistics: vendors, music, food stalls. Hakeem stayed quiet until the subject turned to health and safety. Jada's voice carried steady across the parlor as she laid out plans for a first-aid and wellness booth, hydration stations, maybe even quick mobility checks.

"Good idea," Mr. Willis said. "Folks get to dancing like last year, somebody's gonna twist something again."

Laughter rippled, and Hakeem found himself grinning. He'd forgotten how easily this town laughed together.

Then Ms. Zhang piped up with a twinkle in her eye. "And

maybe we get a warm-up demo! Jada and Mr. Brown here—they know their sports clinics."

Every head seemed to swivel. Hakeem cleared his throat, willing his voice steady. "I can help with that. We can run a short session before the music starts, just basic stretches to keep people loose."

"Oooh, I like that," Rochelle said, jotting notes. "Our star QB and our Dr. Davis, side by side again. Sweetgum's dynamic duo."

Jada's jaw tightened, though she smoothed it over quick. "I'll handle the medical side. If Hakeem wants to lead the demo, that's fine."

He offered her a small, careful smile. "Whatever's needed."

The meeting rolled on—budgets, clean-up crews, vendor confirmations. Hakeem chimed in here and there, but mostly he found his attention tugged sideways. The way Jada carried herself—confident, professional, nothing like the girl who once scribbled his plays on index cards in the bleachers—it made his chest ache. She didn't belong to him anymore, but she sure as hell belonged here.

When Rochelle finally called a break, chairs scraped and folks drifted toward the refreshments. Hakeem made his way to the tea urn, rehearsing a line in his head. *Keep it light. Don't make it weird.*

"Mind if we talk for a sec?" he asked when Jada stepped up.

She hesitated, but nodded.

"I just wanted to say thanks—for not objecting to me helping with the warm-up. I know it's not exactly your dream assignment."

Her voice stayed even, but he heard the steel under it. "We're both here to help Sweetgum. That's all."

He nodded, eyes flicking across the room. "Right. Still. I appreciate it. Last thing I want is to add stress to your life."

Before she could respond, Ms. Zhang swept in with a plate

of scones. "One for each of you—straight from Rochelle's oven. And I can't wait to see your big demo! Maybe you'll dance, too. Didn't you two wow us at the talent show with *Grease*?"

Heat climbed Hakeem's neck. "Uh, yeah. We fumbled through something."

"*Grease*," Jada corrected softly, a hint of a smile tugging at her lips.

"We made it work, though," he said, memory tugging. Then, quickly: "But don't worry, I'm not singing at the festival. Unless you want me to."

That earned him a flicker of amusement, though she kept her tone brisk. "Let's stick to stretches."

They parted when Willis called everyone back to order. The second half of the meeting blurred past: supply lists, booth schedules, final votes. When Rochelle dismissed them, Hakeem lingered in the hall, tugging at the back of his neck—a habit he hated knowing she'd recognize.

She came out with Rochelle, laughing with Benjamin about the lavender trim. When she caught sight of him, her steps slowed.

"You heading out?" he asked.

"I need to type up my supply list," she said, shifting her tote.

"Right." He hesitated, then pushed on. "About the warm-up— I was thinking maybe we could run through it once before the festival. Just to stay in sync."

Her eyes softened, just a shade. "All right. We can schedule something next week."

Relief loosened his shoulders. "Thanks. I'll work around your schedule."

She nodded, already turning toward the door. He found himself blurting, "And Jada?"

She paused, half-turned.

He let out a breath. "I'm looking forward to it."

Her gaze held his a second longer than polite, and her voice was barely above a whisper. "Me too."

As she slipped out into the sunlit street, Hakeem stayed rooted in the hallway, Rochelle's scones perfuming the air, his pulse pounding harder than it had in years. For a simple town festival meeting, it felt like the start of something that might matter more than any stadium ever had.

CHAPTER TWENTY-ONE

*J*ada slipped through the entrance of the familiar diner, letting the comforting aroma of savory food and baked pies settle her nerves.

She hadn't planned on stopping here, but a text from Aimee mentioned:

> Hey, can you swing by the diner? Need a quick word about festival stuff.

Jada figured it'd be a brief chat before she headed home.

A few steps in, she noticed a table of older ladies—Mrs. Bridges, Mrs. Andrews, and Mrs. Craskin—huddled together with half-empty cups of tea. They glanced at her, then quickly resumed chatting, as though they were covering up a momentary hush. Jada pushed aside the ripple of suspicion and wandered to an empty booth near a wide window.

Aimee emerged from the kitchen with a sweet smile. "Dr. Davis, hi! Thanks for coming."

"No problem," Jada said, settling into the booth. She caught sight of Aimee's phone in the younger woman's hand, the screen still glowing from a recent message. "What's up?"

"Just a second." Aimee's gaze darted toward the door. "Let me grab some menus first."

Menus? Jada frowned. *This should be quick, right?* She started to question the reason for the meeting when the diner bell jingled behind her. She glanced back—and froze. Hakeem stood at the threshold, scanning the room. His expression changed from casual to startled the instant he spotted her.

"Oh," he murmured, brow furrowing. "Jada."

She stiffened slightly. "Hakeem. Did… Aimee call you here, too?"

He gave a slow nod, stepping forward. "She mentioned something about the festival. Asked me to swing by on my way home."

Jada's stomach twisted in mild confusion. *Again with the "festival"?* They'd both been volunteering, sure, but this was the third time in a week they'd been summoned somewhere, only to find each other unexpectedly. She fought a flicker of nerves. "Weird."

"Very," Hakeem agreed. He glanced at Aimee, who offered a sheepish wave from behind the counter. "Guess we should, uh, sit?"

She gestured to the opposite seat. "Might as well."

He slid into the booth across from her, knee brace slightly visible beneath his jeans. Small talk buzzed around them— nothing out of the ordinary. Yet Jada couldn't shake the sense of being watched. She noticed how Mrs. Bridges seemed to crane her neck every so often, pretending to check the time on the diner clock.

Aimee returned with menus in hand. "Here you go. On the house if you want some pie or coffee."

Jada blinked. "You're… giving away freebies?"

Aimee's cheeks colored faintly, and she glanced over her shoulder as though worried about being overheard. "Just…just a little thanks for all the festival help you two've done." She rushed off before Jada could probe further.

Hakeem half-laughed, but it was tinged with unease. "Does it feel like we're missing something?"

She drummed her fingers on the table, considering the pattern of "coincidences." They'd been roped into overlapping volunteer shifts. She'd received cryptic texts from random residents. And each time, it ended up with them in the same place, inevitably forced to chat. "Yeah. It's… too coordinated."

They lapsed into silence. Jada sipped water from the glass Aimee had hurriedly set down. She flicked her gaze around the diner again, lingering on the cluster of older women near the corner. A slight hush fell whenever Jada's and Hakeem's eyes roamed that way.

Finally, Hakeem cleared his throat. "You know, I've been meaning to talk to you anyway. Maybe this is as good a time as any."

She braced herself, heart thumping. "Right. You mentioned wanting to clear the air."

A flicker of regret crossed his face. "Yeah. I… I owe you a real apology, Jada. The kind I never gave after high school."

Her chest tightened at the memory of that heartbreak. "Go on," she said softly.

He leaned forward, voice low enough that only she could hear. "I'm sorry I walked away—without letting you weigh in or say anything. I was so focused on a future in the NFL, I convinced myself you'd be better off if we ended things. But not a day went by that I didn't wish I'd handled it differently."

She pressed her lips together, resisting a surge of old pain. "Hakeem, you… I had no idea. For all I knew, you were living it up, forgetting me the second you left."

He shook his head vehemently. "Never. Every touchdown, every city I traveled to, I kept thinking, 'This would be better if

CHAPTER TWENTY-ONE

Jada were here.' And then I'd remember I was the one who shut you out."

She exhaled, struggling to contain the swirl of relief, hurt, and longing. *He missed me? All this time?* Before she could respond, the sudden *ding* of someone's phone made them both glance up. Mrs. Bridges was fiddling with her cell, whispering to Mrs. Andrews, who subtly pointed to Jada and Hakeem's booth.

"Are they… texting about us?" Jada asked under her breath.

Hakeem's brow creased, a slight smile tugging at his lips. "I think so." He paused, understanding dawning in his eyes. "Oh."

They exchanged a look—mutual realization that perhaps *everyone here* was in on something. Mrs. Zhang from across the way offered an awkward wave, then abruptly buried her face in a pamphlet. Meanwhile, Aimee pretended to be cleaning a perfectly clean table, all the while casting sidelong glances at them.

Jada groaned quietly. "They've been setting us up, haven't they? That explains the random shifts, the weird messages about 'urgent' festival business."

Hakeem rubbed a hand over his face. "Looks like it. Half the town must be coordinating."

A momentary burst of laughter from Mrs. Bridges' table gave them all the confirmation they needed. Jada couldn't help a wry chuckle. "Small-town meddling at its finest."

He mirrored her wry amusement, then sobered, returning to the confession he'd started. "I—I know it's not enough for me to just say I'm sorry. But I truly am. I wish I could go back and change everything. I never got over you."

Her heart constricted. "I never got over you either. But I was so angry and hurt that you wouldn't even try."

His voice quavered with remorse. "I was an idiot, thinking that was the best path for both of us. Jada… I'm asking for another chance. If you want it. If you *can* want it."

She fiddled with the edge of a napkin, torn between lingering resentment and a surge of hope. "My head keeps warning me. But my heart… Let's just say it's not over you."

Hakeem gently reached for her hand across the table. "We can take it slow, earn that trust back. Whatever pace you need."

She felt the warmth of his fingers, recalling how that same hand once held hers under stadium lights. "Okay," she murmured, voice shaking. "But if you hurt me again—"

He nodded solemnly. "I won't. I promise."

He squeezed her hand, eyes glinting with earnestness. A hush fell, and Jada realized the entire diner had gone still. Looking around, she saw Mrs. Andrews nudge Mrs. Bridges, while Rochelle, seated with Benjamin in a back booth, half-hidden behind a newspaper, peeked over the top with an excited gleam. Malachi, behind the register, raised an eyebrow as if silently cheering them on.

With a groan-laugh, Jada leaned forward, whispering, "We might be the starring couple in a reality show we never signed up for."

Hakeem laughed softly, shoulders easing. "They mean well. Even if it's a little invasive."

She settled her gaze on him once more, letting the din of the restaurant recede. "So…where do we go from here?"

He cracked a tentative smile. "Maybe we can do a real date soon—where we're not roped into festival duties."

A faint, genuine smile curved her lips. "I'd like that. We can see if the sparks are still there without half the town engineering it."

His eyes lit up. "Tomorrow? Or is that too soon?"

She considered it, heart fluttering. "Tomorrow works. Something casual. Food trucks at the park, maybe?"

He nodded, relief mingled with excitement. "Perfect."

At that moment, Aimee finally ventured back to their booth,

clearing her throat. "Um, not that I'm eavesdropping, but—did you figure out your festival scheduling… or anything else?"

Jada and Hakeem exchanged a look, amusement dancing between them. She answered, "Oh, we figured some things out."

Aimee's face brightened. "That's…great! Then maybe I can bring you the best slice of peach pie to celebrate? On the house, obviously."

Jada smirked, realizing the entire "urgent festival talk" had been a ruse. "Sure. Why not."

Aimee dashed off, beaming. Jada's heart felt both lighter and unsteady—like she'd just made a leap of faith. As she cast one more glance around the diner, she noticed how everyone went back to "casually" minding their own business, though a few proud smiles lingered.

"So," Hakeem said, voice warm with anticipation, "dinner date tomorrow?"

She exhaled softly, nodding. "Yes."

"Thank you," he murmured, not just for the date, but for opening the door he'd slammed shut years before.

She answered with a small, hopeful grin. "Don't make me regret it, Brown."

As their pie arrived, their locked gazes spoke louder than any meddling Auntie's plan. They'd finally discovered the truth: the town had been gently manipulating every overlap and every "coincidence" for weeks. But the realization didn't bother Jada as much as she'd expected. Because in this moment, it felt like maybe—just maybe—they were exactly where they were meant to be.

CHAPTER TWENTY-TWO

Jada stepped onto the gravel path, warm evening air brushing her cheeks. A row of bright string lights wove above the parked food trucks, illuminating hungry patrons who shuffled from window to window in search of barbecue, tacos, or funnel cakes. She clutched her phone, scanning the small crowd.

A flutter of nerves danced in her stomach. This would be her first real date with Hakeem since they were teenagers. *Feels like a lifetime ago,* she thought, recalling the shy way he held her hand at the homecoming fair. Now they were adults, grappling with old heartaches and new hopes.

She spotted him near a neon-lit lemonade stand, leaning against a wooden railing. Even in casual clothes—jeans, T-shirt, a baseball cap—he exuded a quiet confidence. Her gaze flicked to his knee brace, partially hidden but still a reminder of the injury that brought him back to Sweetgum.

When he noticed her approaching, his face lit in a smile that made her chest tighten. "Hey," he said softly, stepping away from the railing. "You look great."

She smoothed the hem of her flowy blouse. "Thanks," she

murmured, taking in the simple sincerity in his eyes. "I'm just glad we're not stuck in some volunteer booth. Feels more… normal."

He chuckled. "Definitely. So… you hungry?"

"Starving," she admitted, glancing at the array of trucks. "This place keeps growing every year. I don't even know where to start."

"Wanna just walk around, see what calls to us?"

She nodded, falling into step beside him. They ambled past a taco truck blasting upbeat music, past a funnel cake cart that filled the air with sweet doughy aromas. The casual closeness brought back flickers of old memories—like how they used to stroll down Sweetgum's Main Street after football games, shoulders brushing, jokes flowing easily.

Now, though, each step felt charged with history. They didn't talk about it directly, but it pulsed in the space between them: *We're trying again. Don't mess this up.*

They paused at a truck selling gourmet grilled cheese sandwiches. Hakeem raised a brow. "Grilled cheese? Classic, but… fancy. Wanna check it out?"

She eyed the menu, smiling at options like "Brie & Pear" or "Cheddar Jalapeño." "I'm game. Let's do it."

While they waited in line, a trio of older ladies ambled past, eyeing them with poorly concealed glee. One even leaned over to whisper something about "so nice to see them out again." Jada felt heat rush to her face, and she cleared her throat, deliberately turning her gaze to the menu.

Hakeem noticed, too. He leaned in. "Guess the entire town's on watch," he murmured.

"Of course they are," she said under her breath, amusement mingled with exasperation. "I'm half expecting a scoreboard around the corner, tracking our progress."

He laughed, a warm, low sound that made her heart lift. "Wouldn't put it past them."

Soon they reached the counter and ordered—Jada picking a Gouda-and-spinach melt, Hakeem opting for a spicy cheddar creation. They stepped aside to wait, the clamor of the crowd a gentle backdrop.

"By the way," Hakeem said, tone turning sincere, "I wanted to ask how your day was—really. Hospital didn't run you ragged?"

She shrugged, recalling a busy morning of patient consultations. "Typical day, honestly. But I do have a new sports rehab case I'm excited about. A sprinter from a neighboring county."

"That's great," he said, genuinely interested. "You've always loved helping athletes bounce back. You were basically the team's secret weapon in high school whenever someone had a twisted ankle."

A wave of nostalgia swept through her. "I remember. Except back then I was just...some girl with a first-aid kit, trying to be useful."

He shook his head. "Nah, you were never 'just some girl.'" His voice softened. "I see that more than ever now."

Her chest fluttered at the earnestness in his gaze. Before she could respond, their names were called. They grabbed the wax-paper-wrapped sandwiches and drifted to a small wooden table under the lights. Settling across from one another, they unwrapped their meals, the savory scents making her stomach growl.

"Wow," Jada breathed, biting into her sandwich. "This is... amazing."

Hakeem grinned around his mouthful of melted cheese. "Better than the cafeteria grilled cheese we used to get, that's for sure."

She smirked, remembering how he used to swipe extra fries from her tray. "Those were tragic. I think that's why we drowned them in ketchup."

They chatted easily as they ate, trading stories about hospital goings-on, his knee rehab progress, and random Sweetgum gossip—like how Ms. Bridges had recently started a crocheting circle that apparently turned into a rumor mill. It felt good, natural, yet tinged with a sense of renewed wonder—like they were rediscovering each other.

Eventually, she leaned back in her chair, taking in the bright strings of lights above. "I still can't believe we're doing this," she admitted, lips curving in a tentative smile. "Feels… surreal."

Hakeem's expression matched the warmth in her voice. "I know. But I'm glad we are." A short silence followed, then he murmured, "Earlier, you asked if we can truly start over. I just want you to know—I'm in this wholeheartedly."

She swallowed, emotions bobbing in her throat. "I'm trying to let myself believe that."

He reached across the table, palm up, inviting her hand. "Take your time. I won't rush."

She stared at his open hand, remembering how she once felt safest when their fingers were entwined. Slowly, she placed her hand in his, letting out a soft, unsteady breath when he laced their fingers together.

A nearby group of teenagers darted by, giggling loudly at something unrelated—but it jolted Jada, pulling her attention. She caught the flicker of curiosity in their eyes, realized they recognized Hakeem from the sports clinics. One boy elbowed another, pointing, and they scurried off with excited whispers.

Hakeem noticed, too, a rueful smile tugging at his lips. "Guess I'll never blend in again, huh?"

She gave his hand a gentle squeeze. "We're in Sweetgum, famous for not letting anything slide under the radar. Especially a second-chance romance."

He breathed out a laugh, eyes alight with something that felt like hope. "Well, if that's our biggest worry, I'll take it."

Jada's chest felt tight in a good way, emotion welling. She realized she might actually be ready to lay down her shields.

"Me too," she whispered, leaning forward. "Thanks for tonight. It...means a lot."

"Thank *you* for giving me a shot," he said earnestly, brushing a thumb over the back of her hand.

They finished their sandwiches in companionable silence, letting the friendly chatter of the food truck crowd swirl around them. As dusk settled, the overhead lights glowed brighter, casting a romantic hue. For once, Jada didn't mind if the entire town saw them like this.

When they stood to toss their wrappers and walk back toward the parking area, she felt more at ease than she had in years. Maybe the meddlesome town had forced their hand, but the truth was, being here with Hakeem felt...right.

He gently guided her around a puddle in the gravel, mindful of her every step. "So, next time," he said as they neared their cars, "I can cook something at my place. I've gotten decent in the kitchen."

Her brows lifted. "You cook now?"

He chuckled. "I had to learn—NFL life doesn't come with a personal chef when you're on the injured list."

She let out a soft laugh. "I'd like that. And I can bring dessert."

His grin brightened. "Deal."

They stopped by her car, the surrounding lamppost casting a warm circle of light. He studied her face, eyes reflecting gratitude and a touch of longing. "Drive safe, Jada."

She nodded, feeling her pulse skip under his gaze. "You too." She hesitated, then leaned in to brush a brief, tentative kiss on his cheek—an echo of affection from the past, now brimming with new possibilities. "See you soon."

Hakeem's breath caught, a slow smile curving his lips. He gently squeezed her hand one last time before stepping back. "Soon," he repeated, voice hushed.

Climbing into her car, Jada felt a swirl of anticipation in her belly. *We're doing this.* The thought of it—really trying—set her heart racing in the most exhilarating way.

She watched him limp slightly toward his own truck, braces hidden beneath denim, but carrying himself with renewed purpose. If the night's tender connection was any sign, their second chance might turn into something stronger than the high school romance they'd once known.

As she pulled away, the glow of the food truck lights receded in the rearview mirror, but a gentle warmth lingered in her chest—hope for what was yet to come.

CHAPTER TWENTY-THREE

Hakeem glanced around his modest living room, heart thumping in anticipation. A faint lemon-and-rosemary aroma drifted in from the kitchen. The scent was warm, inviting—just like he wanted the night to be. He flicked off the overhead light in favor of a soft floor lamp by the couch, hoping the dim glow might ease the nerves twitching in his chest.

Standing by the small dining nook, he smoothed a hand over the tablecloth. Two place settings, fresh daisies in a simple vase, a single candle. Nothing fancy, but he hoped it felt personal, intimate. After so many volunteer meetups and public run-ins, he wanted this night—just the two of them—to show that he was serious about them. *No distractions, no watchful townspeople, just me and her.*

His knee brace pinched slightly against his jeans as he stepped back toward the kitchen. The chicken sizzling in the oven needed basting. Carefully, he opened the oven door, wincing at the blast of heat. *Don't let it burn,* he told himself, drizzling pan juices over the chicken. He could almost hear Jada's teasing voice: *You? Cooking?* A small smile tugged at his mouth. If she teased him for it, he wouldn't mind, as long as she enjoyed the meal.

A light tap at the front door made his pulse kick up a notch. Quickly, he set the basting spoon aside and wiped his hands on a kitchen towel. *This is it. Showtime, Brown.* He crossed the living room, pushing a jitter of nerves aside, and pulled open the door.

Jada stood on the threshold, wearing a simple plum blouse and black jeans, her hair framing her face in soft curls. Her eyes flicked from his face to the warm glow inside, a cautious yet hopeful look shining in them.

"Hey," she said softly, offering a tentative smile. "Something smells incredible."

"Thanks," he managed, stepping back to let her in. "It's, uh, chicken…rosemary-lemon. Still learning my way around spices." A rush of embarrassment flooded him—*former NFL quarterback, and he was fumbling over cooking details.* But the grateful nod she gave him eased that tension immediately.

She slipped off her shoes by the door, taking in the small living room. Hakeem had tidied the couch, folded a throw blanket, even straightened his old football trophies on a shelf. Her gaze lingered there for a moment before traveling back to him. "Nice place," she murmured.

"Thanks," he said, clearing his throat. "It's nothing fancy, but… it's home."

A quiet beat passed, both of them remembering he'd once believed Sweetgum Meadows was too small for him. Now it was all he wanted. He gestured toward the kitchen. "I need to check on the food, but make yourself comfortable, okay?"

She nodded. "Sure." Her gaze trailed him as he headed back to the stove.

Hakeem tried to focus on the last touches of dinner: stirring roasted vegetables, turning off the oven. But every sense buzzed with awareness that Jada was just a few steps away in his living room. The weight of what tonight could mean—proving he was serious about being part of her life—pressed on him in the best possible way. After plating the chicken and veggies, he forced a steady breath. *I can do this.*

He carried the dishes to the table, glancing toward where she stood. She'd wandered closer to his old bookshelf, running fingertips over the spines of novels he'd collected over the years. Something warmed in his chest at the sight—her presence here felt right, as though she belonged.

"All set," he called gently, and she turned with a smile. In the glow of the lamp, she looked breathtaking, every bit the woman he'd never stopped loving.

"Wow," she said, stepping over to him. "You really went all out."

He ducked his head. "It's pretty simple—chicken, veggies. But I wanted to do something special." He gestured to the table. "Hope that's okay."

She rested a hand lightly on the back of one of the chairs. "It's perfect, Hakeem."

The soft sincerity in her voice made his heart twist. Pulling out her chair in a half-teasing, half-genuine gesture, he said, "Trying to be a gentleman here."

She laughed, a low sound that reminded him of easier times. "Thank you."

Once they were seated, Hakeem exhaled, forcing himself to relax. They served themselves, conversation a bit stilted at first —updates about the hospital for her, rehab progress for him. But soon, that familiar rhythm slipped in, each exchange grounded in the comfort they'd once known so well.

"This is delicious," Jada said, after a few bites. A flicker of surprise lit her face. "I'm impressed."

Hakeem felt his cheeks warm. "I had some help from YouTube." He paused, meeting her gaze. "Figured if I can learn to run complicated plays, I can learn to follow a recipe."

She smirked. "I'd call that an excellent use of your strategic mind."

They shared a laugh, and the tension in the air melted into something sweeter, edged with flickering heat. As they ate, the conversation drifted to memories—some funny, like when they snuck into the gym at midnight, convinced security wouldn't catch them practicing a dance routine. Others carried a heavier weight: the night he said goodbye under those stadium lights.

At that mention, a hush fell. Jada set down her fork, and Hakeem's throat constricted. *Don't avoid it,* he told himself. *Face it.*

He laced his fingers, inhaling slowly. "I'm sorry I ever made you feel like you weren't part of my future."

Her lips parted, a soft exhale escaping. "I know. You've said that, but it still hits me sometimes—how final it felt then."

A wave of regret washed over him. He reached out across the table, laying a hand lightly over hers. "Never again," he said, voice barely above a whisper. "I promise."

She studied him, eyes full of unspoken questions, hopes, and maybe lingering fears. But she squeezed his hand, nodding. The electricity of that simple contact pulsed, and he realized how close they were to bridging the last gap of the past.

They finished dinner slowly, each moment crackling with an undercurrent of something that had been building for weeks. When the plates were empty, Hakeem stood to clear them, but Jada rose as well, stepping into his path.

"Let me help," she offered, her tone quiet.

He swallowed, heart thrumming. "You're my guest. It's fine."

She shook her head gently. "We can do it together."

A soft, breathless laugh escaped him. "Okay," he murmured, guiding her to the sink where they set the plates. The closeness, the way she brushed his arm as she reached for a sponge, felt more intimate than any fancy dinner he could have planned.

They washed the few dishes side by side, half-laughing when

a stray sud popped against his chin. Then came the hush—the one where words no longer sufficed. As he handed her a dish to dry, she paused, gaze catching on his face. Heat flared through him, remembering the countless nights he'd lain awake, missing her laughter, her touch, her everything.

"Jada..." Her name slipped from his lips, voice thick.

She set the dish aside, the towel forgotten. "Yeah?" she breathed.

He couldn't stop himself. Stepping forward, he cupped her cheek, thumb brushing the damp corner where a droplet of water clung. She leaned in, eyes fluttering shut. In that instant, the ache of seven lost years ignited into a longing that demanded to be claimed.

He kissed her—soft at first, tasting the faint lemon on her lips, feeling the gentle intake of her breath. She pushed closer, arms wrapping around his shoulders, deepening the contact with a quiet sound that made his blood surge. It was all the pent-up desire, the regret, the hunger for what they used to be and what they could become.

A low warmth coiled through his stomach, and he slipped an arm around her waist, guiding her away from the kitchen sink to the dimly lit living room. She responded with matching fervor, lips parting, letting him pour every unspoken vow into that kiss. There was no hesitation in her now, only a shared urgency that made his heart pound like it used to under Friday night lights.

They broke apart long enough to breathe, foreheads touching. Her eyes shone in the low lamplight, the kind of look that told him she felt it, too—how right this was. Wordlessly, he tangled his fingers in hers, guiding her down the short hallway. With each step, anticipation surged. He heard the whisper of her breath, the quiet rustle of clothing. Every sense blazed.

Moments later, his bedroom door clicked shut behind them. Soft sighs and hushed laughter mingled in the darkness, the final barrier of caution slipping away. It wasn't a frantic reunion but a slow, intense release of all they'd held back. Each caress, each gasp, spoke to the years of separation that had built this longing to a fever pitch.

This time, Hakeem thought between heated kisses and murmured endearments, *this time, I won't let her go.*

A SLIVER of bright sunshine cut through the blinds, hitting Hakeem's eyes. He blinked, disoriented until a gentle weight at his side reminded him of *why* he felt such contentment. Jada lay curled next to him, hair fanned across the pillow. The faint lemony scent from dinner still lingered in the air, mingling with the comforting hush of a new day.

His knee twinged, a physical reminder of how much had changed in his life. He winced, shifting slightly, but the discomfort faded the second Jada stirred. She opened her eyes, gaze meeting his with a hesitant, sleepy smile.

"Morning," she whispered, voice low and raspy.

His chest fluttered with a mix of tenderness and relief. "Morning," he echoed, brushing a stray curl from her face. "You okay?"

She nodded, her cheeks coloring faintly. "Yeah. I am." A quiet pause, then she added with a small laugh, "Didn't expect to stay the night, but…"

He tightened his arm around her waist. "I'm glad you did." The memory of last night thrummed through him, a heady mix of passion and yearning finally answered. He trailed a thumb gently over her arm, feeling the warmth of her skin. "I, um… hope you don't regret it."

She let out a slow breath, eyes flicking over his face as if searching for something. "No," she said quietly. "No regrets. Just…realizing we still have to figure out where this goes."

His throat constricted. "We will. Together." He fought the surge of fear that threatened. There were still obstacles—his looming NFL question, her lingering worries about him leaving again. But for now, her presence beside him felt like the promise of a real future.

Her lips curved into a gentle smile. "I believe you."

They lay there a moment longer, content in the hush of early morning. Finally, she sat up, pulling the sheet around her. The sunlight highlighted the graceful line of her shoulders, making his heart clench with reverence. He eased himself upright, shifting his brace, grateful for how far they'd come.

As she rubbed sleep from her eyes, a playful grin tugged at her lips. "So…did you plan to serve me breakfast, too, Chef Hakeem?"

He laughed, the sound echoing softly in the room. "I can whip up some scrambled eggs, if you trust me in the kitchen again."

She leaned over, brushing a tender kiss to his cheek. "I'd like that."

In that quiet moment, with morning light spilling across the rumpled bed, Hakeem felt the last vestiges of doubt fade. Whatever challenges lay ahead—whether with football, therapy, or the shadows of their past—he wasn't facing them alone this time. They'd reclaimed what they'd lost, and maybe, just maybe, had found something even stronger.

He squeezed her hand, determination flooding him. He wouldn't let fear derail them again. If last night proved anything, it was that their connection still burned bright. And as she offered a sleepy, radiant smile, Hakeem silently vowed to protect that flame with every ounce of love he had.

CHAPTER TWENTY-FOUR

The aroma of scrambled eggs pulled Jada from the haze of half-sleep. Last night's surge of longing, the tentative confessions, the slow unraveling of years' worth of distance: it all converged into a heady swirl of memories that made her cheeks flush.

Sitting up, she ran a hand through her hair, trying to tame the wild curls. She spotted her clothes folded neatly on a nearby chair, and a faint laugh escaped her. *Hakeem actually folded them.* She never imagined he'd be so thoughtful about tiny details; teenage Hakeem might've tossed them aside without a second thought.

Slipping out of bed, she stretched, rolling her shoulders. A dull ache in her muscles reminded her of their passionate night, and a shy thrill ignited at the base of her spine. *Get it together, Jada—time to face the morning.* She quickly went to freshen up. She then dressed, smoothing down her blouse, before venturing into the hallway.

She found him in the kitchen, braced knee peeking beneath loose gray sweatpants. He was focused on the stove, spatula in hand. Light from the narrow window caught his profile: sharp jawline, steady brow. A flutter tugged at her chest.

He glanced over his shoulder and smiled. One that seemed to radiate from deep within. "Hey, you. Sleep okay?"

She padded across the small living room, leaning against the kitchen doorway. "Better than okay," she admitted, voice husky. "Though your bed could use an upgrade in the pillow department."

A low chuckle rumbled in his throat. "Noted. Maybe you can help me pick out new ones." He gently stirred the eggs, then lowered the heat. "I was about to wake you, but...figured you might need some rest after...you know."

A blush threatened. She cleared her throat, glancing at the countertop. There were already plates out, a small jar of jam, and slices of toast. He really was going all out with domestic flair. "This is...nice," she murmured. "I'm usually grabbing breakfast on the go."

"Figured we deserved a slow morning," he said. Then, more softly, "If...that's okay with you?"

Jada's heart thudded. "Yeah." She stepped closer, tentatively slipping her arms around his waist. He stilled, turning to face her fully. In the morning light, she could see the careful mixture of affection and uncertainty in his eyes—like he was waiting for a sign she didn't regret anything.

She rose up on her tiptoes and pressed a kiss to his cheek, letting her fingers brush the back of his neck. "I'm not in a rush," she whispered.

A quiet exhale of relief left him. He set the spatula down, returning her embrace. "Me neither."

They stood there for a moment, a hush of newly formed intimacy washing over them. Through the window, she spotted the houses of Sweetgum in the distance—neighbors probably already gossiping about her car parked outside Hakeem's place all night. The thought coaxed a laugh from her lips.

"What's funny?" he asked, pulling back just enough to see her face.

She shook her head. "Just...wondering how quickly word will spread that I never went home last night."

A rueful grin tugged his mouth. "Probably half the town knows by now. If I had to guess, Rochelle already told Mrs. Zhang, and Ms. Bridges overheard." He paused, shrugging. "Strangely enough, I don't mind."

Her stomach fluttered. "Me neither."

He brushed a gentle kiss against her temple, then turned to scoop the eggs onto plates. "C'mon, let's eat before everything gets cold."

They settled at the small table, legs bumping under the surface as they adjusted to the close space. She savored each bite of fluffy eggs, the comfortable hush allowing a sense of normalcy to blossom—like they'd been doing this for years, instead of it being their first morning truly "together."

At one point, she caught him staring, and her heart flip-flopped. "What?" she asked, cheeks warming.

"Nothing," he murmured, lifting his coffee cup. "Just...glad you're here."

Her chest clenched with a gentle ache. "Me too."

After breakfast, they cleared the dishes, working around each other with practiced ease. The moment felt almost domestic—an odd contrast to the heartbreak they'd once endured. She couldn't help but think how different life might've been if he'd never left, if they'd stuck it out after high school. But as soon as the pang of regret hit, she pushed it aside. *No point dwelling on what-ifs. They had now—and that was enough.*

He set a towel on the counter, wiping his hands. "So, I know you probably have a shift soon. Need me to drop you off to your car?"

She glanced at the time on her phone. "Yeah, I do have to be at the hospital in a couple hours, but I drove here. My car's parked out front."

Relief softened his expression. "Right. Of course."

She could practically feel the unspoken tension: neither of them wanted this morning to end. But life called. *We'll be normal people with normal routines,* she told herself, though a grin tugged at her lips at how *not normal* this felt, after so many years apart.

He must've felt it too, because he walked her to the door with an almost shy hesitation. "Hey," he murmured, once they reached the threshold. "You're still good for that date tomorrow, right? The nature walk by the lake?"

Warmth flared in her chest. They'd planned a casual weekend outing—a small step further into a real relationship. "Absolutely," she said.

He cupped her cheek, pressing a tender kiss to her forehead. The brush of his lips sent a pleasant hum through her body, recalling flashes of last night's intensity. It took every ounce of professionalism not to linger, but she forced herself to step back.

"See you soon," she whispered, heart pounding. With one last smile, she slipped out into the sunlight, heading toward her car.

JADA NAVIGATED THE BUSY CORRIDOR, mind half on her patients, half on the morning she'd just shared. As she prepped for her next consult, she couldn't help imagining the wave of gossip likely brewing. Still, she felt a calm contentment. *Let them talk,* she thought.

Inside her small office, she tapped at her computer, updating digital files for new sports therapy patients. Her phone buzzed, drawing her attention. A text from Hakeem lit the screen:

CHAPTER TWENTY-FOUR

Good luck with the shift. Knee is feeling good,
thanks to you. See you tomorrow, beautiful.

A rush of warmth spread from her chest outward. She typed a quick reply—

Same. Behave yourself, Brown.

—and tucked her phone away, biting down a grin.

Moments later, a knock on her office door made her jolt. She pasted on a professional smile. "Come in."

An older nurse, Inez, stepped inside, eyebrows raised. "Dr. Davis, that teen patient from last week, Jeremy, is here. Says he wants to double-check his PT routine."

"Sure," Jada said, standing. "I'll walk with you."

They headed down the hallway, past bustling staff and visitors. Inez glanced at Jada with a coy look. "So… hear you're looking mighty happy these days," she said, half-singing the words.

Jada stifled a laugh. *So it begins.* "Rumors fly fast around here, Inez."

"Mm-hmm," the nurse teased, tapping her pen on the clipboard. "But you know us. We love to see folks find a little joy, especially with an old flame."

Heat prickled Jada's cheeks, but an undeniable sense of contentment filled her. "I appreciate your concern," she said diplomatically.

Inez chuckled. "If you need me to hush folks up, just let me know. Otherwise, I think everyone's rooting for you."

With that, they stopped in front of Jeremy's room, conversation shifting to the teen's progress. Jada refocused on her work, but her heart remained light. Even with the small-town meddling, she found she didn't mind. She had Hakeem's gentle grin fresh in her memory, and that was enough to keep her spirits buoyed.

RETURNING HOME AFTER HER SHIFT, Jada shrugged off her coat, dropping her keys on the kitchen counter. She glanced around her modest studio, still peppered with unpacked boxes she never quite finished organizing. *I might have a reason to do that now,* she thought, a surge of motivation flickering—*especially if we become more serious.* The idea of "sharing space" with him in the future crossed her mind, and a swirl of nerves followed.

To distract herself, she took out ingredients for a quick dinner. Her phone chimed with a call from her mom, which she answered on speaker as she chopped vegetables.

"Hey, Mom," she greeted, trying to keep her tone casual.

"Hi, sweetheart," came her mother's warm voice. "Heard through the grapevine you've been spending time with that Brown boy again. You okay?"

Jada huffed out a breath, adding peppers to a sizzling pan. "Word does travel fast."

Her mom laughed softly. "Might've come from Missus Bridges. Or Missus Andrews. Or both."

Jada shook her head, a fond exasperation tugging at her lips. "I'm fine, Mom. We're… dating. It's new, but it feels right."

A brief pause followed, then her mother said, "I'm happy for you, Jada. I know how much you loved him back then—and how badly it hurt. Just be careful, okay?"

"Mom," Jada murmured, stirring the pan, "I promise, I'm being careful. But… I do feel good about it."

Her mom sighed in relief. "That's all I need to hear. Daddy sends his love."

They exchanged a few more pleasantries before hanging up. Jada finished cooking, a sense of peace drifting over her despite the day's bustle. The thought of tomorrow's date—Hakeem and the lake, maybe a quiet walk—made her chest flutter with anticipation.

She settled down at her small two-person table, mind meandering to how drastically life had shifted in just a few weeks. *We went from avoiding each other to sharing breakfast. From heartbreak to...something real.* She couldn't help a hopeful smile. Sure, they had challenges to face—Hakeem's future in or out of the NFL, her lingering wariness. But for tonight, she let contentment wrap around her like a soft blanket.

Flicking off the kitchen light, she stepped into her bedroom, new possibilities humming in her thoughts. If the morning after was any sign, they were on the right path—together, at last.

CHAPTER TWENTY-FIVE

$\mathcal{H}$akeem wiped his brow, the midday sun beating down on the open field. He paused mid-task, leaning the pitchfork against the fence, and stretched his leg to relieve the brace's pressure. Working around the family dairy farm had become part of his rehab routine—helping Rashad with chores while building back muscle strength.

Sometimes, as he trudged between hay bales and feed bags, his mind drifted to the old fantasies he once held—blazing stadium lights, roaring crowds. Yet these days, a quieter future here in Sweetgum felt more tempting than any distant field.

Just as he picked up the pitchfork again, his phone buzzed in his pocket. Grunting, he tugged off a glove and retrieved the phone. The screen showed an unknown number. *Spam?* he wondered, but curiosity prodded him to answer.

"Hello?" he said, stepping a few paces away from the cow enclosure, where Rashad was busy adjusting a gate.

"Is this Hakeem Brown?" came a confident male voice on the line. "I'm calling on behalf of the Houston Fury—heard you're doing well with your rehab."

Hakeem's heart lurched, recognition slamming into him. *An*

NFL call? Seriously? Clearing his throat, he fought to steady his voice. "Y-yes, this is Hakeem. I'm…surprised to hear from you."

"We've got an eye on a few free agents, especially those recovering from injuries," the man explained. "We caught wind that your knee's on track for full clearance soon. Wanted to see where you stand on returning to the league—maybe even do a private workout to gauge your status."

A rush of adrenaline threaded with anxiety pulsed through him. He glanced at the knee brace. *So the league is still paying attention, huh?* For a second, a younger version of himself roared with excitement, imagining stepping back under those lights. But an image of Jada's face flicked into his mind, soft and full of trust.

He inhaled. "I'm honored you'd reach out. I, uh, didn't realize my progress was on your radar."

"We like to keep tabs on promising players," the man said smoothly. "No pressure, but we'd love to set something up in the next few weeks if you're open."

Hakeem swallowed, his mouth suddenly dry. "Let me think about it. My doctors and PT still have me on a schedule. I… haven't made any final decisions yet."

"Understood," the man replied. "I'll follow up in a week or so. We'd hate to see your talent off the field for good."

With that, the call ended. Hakeem stood there, phone clutched tight, a swirl of conflicting emotions whirling inside him. Part of him felt that old, fierce spark of ambition. Another part clenched with unease. *What about Jada? She's finally trusting me not to leave. And here's the NFL calling again?*

"Everything okay?" came Rashad's voice from behind.

Hakeem turned to see his older brother, dusty from farm work, brow knitted in concern. "Yeah," Hakeem managed. "Just got a call from an NFL rep. Wants me to consider returning."

Rashad's eyebrows shot up. "That's big news. Are you… interested?"

Hakeem stared at the farmhouse in the distance, remembering the nights he'd convinced himself Sweetgum was too small. Now, the thought of leaving Jada, of uprooting what they'd rebuilt, sent a cold pinch of dread through him. "I'm not sure," he admitted quietly. "My knee's doing better, but—Jada and I just got back on track. I don't want to risk losing her again."

Rashad set down his own tools, eyes understanding. "I get it. But you also worked your whole life for that dream. Don't you at least owe it to yourself to see if you can still play?"

Conflicting emotions tangled in Hakeem's gut. "I guess so," he said eventually. "But I'm torn. Football was my everything. Now… Jada's more important than any spotlight. If going back means losing her, I can't do that."

Rashad clapped him on the shoulder. "You know her best, man. Jada's strong, but she's also been hurt before—by you leaving. If you decide to consider this, be honest with her. Don't blindside her."

Hakeem nodded, chest tight. "Yeah. Honesty this time."

With a heavy sigh, he pocketed his phone. The farm chores beckoned, but his thoughts remained fixed on that phone call, tension creeping into every breath. *So much for a calm morning.*

Hours later, after finishing up at the farm, Hakeem drove into town with half-formed plans to catch Jada at lunch. He still wore his work boots and the brace under his jeans. Normally, he'd have changed into something cleaner, but his mind buzzed too loudly to focus on small details. *I just need to talk to her.*

He parked near the hospital, a sense of déjà vu hitting him. He'd come here months ago, broken in spirit, not realizing Jada worked as a physical therapist. Now, everything was different, yet somehow on the verge of the same threat—him leaving.

Calm down, Brown. He swallowed the knot in his throat. He wouldn't let old mistakes haunt them.

Climbing out of the truck, he spotted her across the street, grabbing a sandwich from a small kiosk near the hospital entrance. She looked up just as he approached, surprise lighting her face. "Hakeem? Everything okay?"

He noticed concern flickering in her gaze, and his heart twisted at how quickly she read him. "I—sorry, I just…" He forced a steady exhale. "Do you have a minute?"

She glanced at her watch. "My next appointment isn't for twenty minutes. Walk with me?"

He nodded, matching her pace as she headed around the corner to a quieter bench near the side of the hospital. The bench faced a small garden patch, a green respite among concrete. Setting her sandwich on her lap, she turned to him, eyes gentle yet searching. "What's on your mind?"

His pulse pounded. He remembered his vow to be honest— no more secrets. "I got a call today," he began, voice low. "From an NFL team. Houston Fury. They heard about my knee recovery and…they want me to consider coming back."

Her expression shifted from curiosity to a guarded kind of fear. "That's…big. I, um—" She licked her lips. "Did they offer you a contract right away?"

"No, just a workout invitation," he clarified. "But you know how it goes—if they're calling, it's pretty serious interest." He paused, voice tightening. "I don't want you to think I'm about to bail on Sweetgum. I'm not. I just…didn't want to hide this from you."

She glanced down at her uneaten sandwich, tension in the set of her shoulders. "Thank you for telling me," she said softly. A moment passed as she processed it. "How do you feel about it?"

Hakeem ran a hand through his hair, frustration brimming. "Conflicted. Football was my dream. But after everything… I don't want to lose you. I don't want you to think I'm picking the NFL over us."

The raw note in his voice made her set the sandwich aside, turning fully toward him. "Hakeem, it's your dream. I'd never ask you to give it up just for me. But…" Her voice wavered. "I can't pretend it doesn't scare me. You left once before for football."

He swallowed, guilt biting deep. "I know. That's why I'm— I don't want to go unless we figure out a way that works for both of us, if I even decide to go at all."

A slight breeze rustled the leaves of the garden patch. Jada's eyes shone with a swirl of emotions. "I don't want to be the reason you regret not trying," she whispered. "But I also don't want to be left behind again."

The vulnerability in her words hit him like a punch. He reached for her hand, relieved when she let him take it. "I won't repeat the past," he said firmly. "If I do this, it's with you—on our terms. Or not at all."

She studied him for a long breath, then nodded, the tightness in her posture easing just a fraction. "Okay," she murmured. "We talk this through, see what your doctors say, see what we can handle. Together."

Relief swept through him, though the anxiety lingered beneath. "Thank you," he breathed. "I'm not sure if I even want that life anymore. But it felt wrong not telling you."

She gave a weak smile. "I appreciate the honesty." Her tone gentled. "We'll figure it out. Just… one day at a time. Maybe you go to the workout and see how it feels?"

He squeezed her hand, gratitude coursing through him. "One day at a time," he repeated, a fresh wave of devotion flooding him. *She's giving me the freedom to decide, even though she's scared.* He vowed then to never take that trust for granted.

She glanced at her watch, letting out a reluctant sigh. "I have to get back. Appointment starts soon."

He stood with her, heart feeling both heavy and hopeful. "I'll call you later, okay?"

She nodded, and before he could second-guess himself, he leaned in to press a gentle kiss to her temple, ignoring the passerby who might be watching. "Take care," he murmured.

Her lips curved in a shaky smile. "You too."

With that, she headed back to the hospital, leaving Hakeem on the bench, phone still clutched tight. He gazed at the garden, thoughts tangling. A shot at returning to the NFL was everything he'd once wanted. Now, it felt like a threat to the happiness he'd only just reclaimed. *One day at a time, Brown. Don't lose sight of what matters most.*

He inhaled the crisp air, determined to handle this with the care he'd never shown before. If he was going to face the NFL again, he'd do it with Jada at his side—or not at all.

CHAPTER TWENTY-SIX

Cool morning air brushed across Jada's arms as she stepped onto the narrow lakeside trail. Rays of early sunlight danced on the water's surface, creating shimmering patterns that reminded her of childhood summers. Hakeem had suggested a nature walk here—a casual date that wouldn't strain his knee but would still let them enjoy some quiet time. *And maybe talk about that NFL call,* she thought, nerves fluttering.

She glanced behind to see Hakeem approach. Even through the soft hush of the morning, she noticed the heavy set of his shoulders, the wary look in his eyes that betrayed the weight he carried.

"Beautiful spot," she said when he caught up, forcing a lightness to her voice. "I forgot how peaceful it is this early."

He nodded, gaze wandering over the lake's rippling expanse. "Yeah, it's been a while since I came out here. Figured it'd be a good place to…clear our heads."

Her heart twisted at the subtle hint. *Clear our heads about the NFL scare.* They walked side by side, the dirt path crunching beneath their feet. The mild tension lingered, a gentle reminder that, though they'd reconnected, they were still navigating fragile ground.

"Your knee okay?" she asked quietly, noticing a slight hitch in his gait.

He shrugged, flexing the brace. "A little stiff, but manageable. Probably from farm work and the extra therapy exercises." A brief smile touched his mouth. "No condemnation from my PT, please."

She snorted softly. "I'll hold back—for now." Though she tried for humor, her chest still felt tight. *He's healing physically, but what about us emotionally?*

They continued along the trail until they reached a small wooden bench perched under a willow tree. She gestured for him to sit, a subtle nudge that *yes, you can rest.* He obliged, and she settled beside him, letting the quiet of the lake fill the silence.

For a moment, neither spoke, just watching a pair of ducks glide across the water. Finally, Hakeem sighed. "I keep running that phone call through my head," he admitted. "Part of me feels…curious, I guess. Like, do I still have it in me? Could I go back?"

Jada clasped her hands on her lap, gaze on the shimmering lake. "Of course you wonder," she said gently. "You worked your whole life to get to the NFL."

He nodded. "But I also remember what that life was like—constant travel, intense pressure. And now there's you." His voice dropped, thick with tenderness. "I can't picture leaving you behind again, even if it's for a contract."

Warmth and worry tangled in her chest. She reached over, resting a hand lightly on his. "You wouldn't necessarily have to leave me behind. People do long-distance, or I could—" She trailed off, the words tasting uncertain on her tongue. She loved her job, her life here. And deep down, the idea of uprooting everything for him ignited old wounds: *He left me once—why should I chase him a second time?*

"You could...what?" he prompted, turning his hand to thread their fingers.

Her lips flattened as she stared at their linked hands. "I don't know," she said quietly. "But if you do a workout, if they offer you a place on the roster... we'd have to talk about what that means for us. I can't pretend it wouldn't scare me."

He swallowed, his grip tightening around her fingers. "I hate that I put you in this position again," he murmured, regret carving lines into his face. "I wish the choice were simple."

Jada inhaled slowly, letting the crisp air fill her lungs. "Look...I don't want you to resent me for not trying. Or resent the NFL for taking you from me. We have to figure out if there's a middle ground."

He nodded, glancing at a passing duck quacking at the water's edge. "Rashad thinks I should at least see if I can handle a workout. Whether I can physically hold up in a real practice environment. I told the rep from the Fury I'd get back to him in a week." He paused, shifting his brace. "Maybe I do it. If it feels wrong or my knee acts up, we know it's not an option."

A stab of cold fear mingled with reluctant acceptance in her belly. She fought to keep her tone steady. "That might be the only way to know for sure. Otherwise, you'll always wonder."

He angled toward her, capturing her gaze. "You're not mad?"

A gentle pang echoed in her chest. "I'm not... *mad.* Maybe I'm anxious. But I told you, I don't want you regretting not trying." She let out a shaky breath. "Just promise me we'll talk about every step. No shutting me out."

The flash of gratitude in his eyes tugged at her heart. "I promise," he said firmly, bringing her hand to his lips for a soft kiss. "No more secrets, no more big decisions without you."

Jada's throat tightened. She believed him—and that belief felt both comforting and terrifying. "We'll get through it," she whispered, leaning her head briefly on his shoulder. For a while, they just sat there, the gentle lap of water against the shore mingling with the rustle of willow branches overhead.

~

THEY'D BROUGHT SIMPLE SNACKS—SANDWICHES, bottled water. After the tense talk, they agreed to keep enjoying the day, choosing a sunny patch on the grassy bank for a makeshift picnic. Jada spread out a small blanket, and Hakeem reclined beside her, propping himself on an elbow.

She offered him half of her sandwich, and he raised an eyebrow. "Turkey and avocado?"

She shrugged. "Best the café had this morning. I kind of rushed out."

He took a bite, letting out a quiet hum of approval. "Better than my cooking."

She gave him a playful nudge with her shoulder. "Your cooking was pretty great, actually."

A flicker of warmth lit his eyes, and her mind raced back to the intensity of their shared night in his bed. Her cheeks heated slightly, but she refused to shy away from the memory. *We belong together now, so there's no shame in it.*

As if sensing her thoughts, he set the sandwich aside. Gently, he reached for her hand, interlacing their fingers. Her chest tightened with a mix of longing and tenderness. The wind stirred the grass, carrying the faint scent of pine and water.

"Could do this every day," he murmured, voice tinged with wonder. "Sit by the lake, talk about… anything. Feels right."

She smoothed her thumb along his knuckles. "Yeah," she breathed. "It does." Despite the looming NFL question, in this moment, everything felt blissfully simple.

He leaned closer, pressing a soft kiss to her temple. The gesture was tender, lacking the urgency of previous nights but infused with a steady devotion that made her heart ache in the best way.

Just then, a splash of water drew their attention. Down by the shoreline, a pair of teenagers in swimsuits laughed, splashing each other. They caught sight of Hakeem, eyes going wide, and one boy exclaimed, "Yo! That's Hakeem Brown, right?" He elbowed his friend, pointing excitedly.

Jada stifled a laugh as the boys hurried over, dripping water along the grass. "Dude, I watched all your college highlights," one said, breathless. "You really in Sweetgum now?"

Hakeem cleared his throat, a grin tugging at his mouth. "Yep. Been back a while."

"That's sick! Are you going back to the league?" the other boy asked, eyes shining. "Heard rumors you might."

A pang shivered through Jada. She squeezed Hakeem's hand, and he responded with a subtle squeeze of reassurance. "Not sure yet, guys," he told them lightly. "Focusing on my knee first."

They nodded, still brimming with excitement. "We gotta get a photo with you," the first boy said. "People won't believe this."

With a bemused chuckle, Hakeem obliged, and the teens snapped a quick selfie. After a chorus of thanks, they scurried off, leaving a hush in their wake.

Jada let out a slow breath. "You're kind of a legend, you know."

He gave a wry shrug, sliding an arm around her waist. "Maybe a small-town legend. Guess I forgot what it felt like to have folks see me as 'the athlete' instead of just...me."

She laid her head against his shoulder. "For what it's worth, I prefer the 'just you' version."

His grip tightened around her, affection coloring his voice. "Then that's who I'll keep being."

They fell silent again, the sun inching higher in the sky. Despite the knot of worry about the future, Jada felt a glimmer of relief that they'd addressed the NFL possibility openly. If he did attempt a workout, at least she'd be in the loop—*they'd be in it together.*

Eventually, Hakeem helped her up, his knee brace creaking slightly. She gathered the trash, he folded the blanket. Once they were done, they lingered at the water's edge, gazing out over the tranquil ripples.

"How about we head back?" she suggested, voice soft. "I've got some errands. But… maybe dinner tomorrow? We can cook at my place this time."

He smiled. "I'd love that."

As they walked hand in hand toward the parking area, Jada's steps felt lighter than they had that morning. Sure, the conversation about the NFL had stirred fear, but it also solidified their determination to face it head-on—no secrets, no half-measures.

She glanced sideways at him, warmth blooming in her chest. *We're stronger together than we ever were apart.* And as the day's golden light spilled across their path, she silently thanked whatever meddling force in Sweetgum had pushed them back into each other's orbit, determined never to waste a second chance at the love they'd once lost.

CHAPTER TWENTY-SEVEN

*H*akeem stood at his kitchen counter, phone pressed to his ear, heart pounding. Outside, the last streaks of sunset painted the horizon in gold and pink, but he barely noticed. The voice on the other end belonged to the Houston Fury rep, polite and professional, detailing a potential date for a private workout.

"Yes, sir," Hakeem said quietly, glancing down at his knee brace. "That date could work. Let me just confirm with my PT and see if I can get a few days in Houston."

A slight surge of adrenaline rippled through him. *This is real.* His mind flashed to old triumphs—spiraling passes, roaring crowds, every dream he'd ever had about football. But right on its heels came the memory of Jada's anxious eyes, the vow he'd made that they'd decide together.

"Understood," said the rep. "We'll email you details. Looking forward to seeing you in action again."

"Right," Hakeem murmured. "Thank you." With that, the call ended.

He exhaled, shoulders tensing. *I told Jada I'd keep her in the loop.* The exercise in honesty felt unfamiliar but necessary, like a muscle he was just learning to use.

Gathering his courage, he tapped open his messages. *She said she'd be cooking at her place tonight.* He typed a quick note:

> Hey, can I come over a little earlier than we planned? Got an update on that NFL thing.

He hit send and braced a hand against the counter, trying to steady his breathing. The thought of picking up a football in a professional setting again stirred up conflicting emotions—a blend of excitement and dread. *Is it too late to back out?* he wondered. But the recruiter's confidence in him reminded Hakeem of the unstoppable teen who once believed he was meant to conquer the league.

A minute later, Jada's reply buzzed in:

> Sure. I'm home now, slicing veggies. Whenever you're ready.

He grabbed his keys and headed out, ignoring the nagging pinch in his knee. *Better let her see the brace today, no bravado.* If he was truly ready for an NFL workout, he needed full honesty about his body's condition, not just with Jada but also with himself.

He climbed the narrow staircase, the aroma of sautéing onions drifting through the slightly ajar door. Nerves fluttered. *Relax, Brown. You promised to talk everything out.* He knocked lightly, pushing the door open at her call of "Come in!"

Her cozy studio greeted him with warm lamplight. Jada stood by the kitchenette, wearing a casual T-shirt and leggings, hair pinned up. She shot him a quick smile as she worked a wooden spoon through a pan of sizzling peppers.

"Hey," she said softly. "Everything okay? You look stressed."

He nodded, stepping out of his shoes. "Just... dealing with the NFL rep. They, uh, want me in Houston in a couple weeks for a workout." He paused, meeting her gaze. "I told him I'd confirm after talking with you and my PT."

She studied him, turning off the stovetop. Her eyes flicked to his knee brace. "So it's getting real, huh?"

He huffed a brittle laugh. "Real enough that I'm feeling that old adrenaline. But also a million doubts."

Moving from behind the counter, she motioned him to the small table. "Have a seat. Let's talk." Her voice was calm, but he caught the slight tremor underneath.

He sank into one of the chairs, resting an elbow on the table. She joined him, folding her hands in her lap. The hush between them felt thick. In the background, the steady hiss of the stovetop died away, replaced by a gentle hum of the fridge.

"So, two weeks," she said, brows knitting. "That's soon. Do you think your knee can handle it?"

He ran a hand over his brace. "I'm making progress, but I'll push a little harder in therapy to be sure. I'll talk to you in your professional capacity, of course, as well as in your personal capacity." A hint of a wry smile curved his lips. "If that's okay."

She looked torn between amusement and worry. "I'm game, but you also have Dr. Hayes for the official sign-off."

"Yeah." He exhaled. "I guess my question is: if the doctor says I can handle this, and the Fury sees potential, what then? Do I... move? Do we try long-distance? I said I wouldn't run off on you, but an NFL contract's no small commitment."

Her expression tightened. "You said we'd figure it out together. I meant that. I won't stand in your way, but I—I'm scared it'll be the same story, me alone in Sweetgum, you chasing stadium lights." She paused, dropping her gaze. "I don't want to feel like the second choice again."

Pain speared his chest. He gently reached over, covering her hand with his. "You're not second choice. I don't even know if I *want* that life anymore. But a part of me thinks I owe it to myself to at least see."

She lifted her eyes, the worry there softened by acceptance. "Then do it. Do the workout. Let's see how it feels, physically and emotionally. If it's everything you remember, maybe we find a way. If it's not..." She trailed off, swallowing.

"Then I stay," he finished quietly. "Here, with you."

Her lips quirked in a sad smile. "Yeah."

For a long moment, they sat in that tense hush. Then she squared her shoulders, shifting gears. "All right. That's decided. You'll do the workout, I'll help you prep physically. We keep talking about every step. No big leaps alone."

He nodded, relief flooding him at her steadiness. "No leaps alone," he echoed. "Thank you, Jada."

She rose from the chair, inhaling as though clearing her head. "Well, we can talk details after dinner. I hope you like stir-fry," she said, attempting a lighter tone.

He stood, catching her hand before she could slip away. "Stir-fry's perfect," he murmured, voice low with gratitude. "And...you're amazing."

Her cheeks colored faintly, eyes flicking to where their fingers intertwined. "I'm just... trying not to freak out," she admitted, a tremulous laugh escaping. "But we'll manage. We have to."

The honesty cut through him, and an urge to reassure her in more than words flared. He dipped his head, pressing a tender kiss to the back of her hand. "We will," he whispered.

She let out a shaky breath, returning a soft kiss on his cheek before gently pulling free. "Okay, let's get this stir-fry done before we burn the apartment down." Her smile was small but determined.

THEY SAT at her modest table, steaming bowls of stir-fry between them. The sweet-savory aroma filled the cozy space, and Hakeem's chest lightened. The simple act of sharing a meal with her, talking about daily life—like which volunteer events needed coverage or how her new sports rehab patient was progressing—made him marvel at how lucky he felt, even amid the looming uncertainty.

Midway through the meal, his phone vibrated on the table. He glimpsed the screen: a text from Dr. Hayes' office, confirming an upcoming checkup. *It's all moving fast,* he thought, heart pounding. *Focus on the now.*

"So," Jada said, drawing him back. "After dinner, you want to set up a quick therapy schedule for the next week? We can incorporate extra strength drills for your knee."

He nodded, surprised at how comforting the suggestion felt. "Yeah, that'd help. The stronger I go into that workout, the clearer my head will be."

She shot him a level look. "Don't push too hard. We want you healthy, not re-injured."

A wave of warmth coursed through him. *She cares so fiercely.* "I'll be careful. Especially with you watching over me, Doc."

She couldn't hold back a grin. "That's right. I take my job seriously."

They polished off the stir-fry, the conversation weaving between everyday banter and the heavier undercurrent of potential changes. When the plates were empty, he insisted on helping with the dishes, relishing the domestic tranquility of washing and drying side by side.

THEY ENDED up on her small couch, some low music playing from her phone's speaker. He rested an arm along the couch back, drawing her close enough that she leaned into him, her head at his shoulder. Outside, night had fully fallen, the hush of Sweetgum wrapping around them.

He let out a content sigh. *This is what I've always wanted—peace, closeness, no regrets.* Except for the small voice reminding him that in two weeks, everything could change.

"I was thinking," Jada murmured, breaking his reverie. "You should do some field drills at the high school—test how your knee feels moving laterally, pivoting. See if you get any pain."

He rubbed a hand over her arm. "That's a good idea. Maybe tomorrow afternoon?"

She nodded, tilting her face up. "I can carve out time after the hospital if you want me there."

A wave of gratitude and affection welled in him. "I do," he said simply. "I'd feel better having you watch me, see if I'm pushing too far."

Her eyes flicked with warmth. "We'll figure it out," she repeated, giving his shirt a gentle tug to draw him into a tender kiss. The warmth of her lips against his made every doubt fade momentarily.

He deepened the kiss, mindful of the brace, hoping to convey all the emotions he couldn't quite put into words. When she pulled back, cheeks flushed, a shy smile curved her mouth. "Thank you for not shutting me out," she whispered.

His chest tightened with love and remorse for the past. "Never again," he vowed softly, pressing his forehead to hers.

They lingered like that, enveloped in a quiet sense of trust. He realized that no matter what happened with the NFL, the real victory was here—building a life with the only person he'd ever truly wanted by his side.

As he left her apartment an hour later, he felt a surge of

resolve. *He'd do the workout, but he wouldn't let it define him.* If his knee or his heart told him it wasn't right, he'd walk away without regret. Because for the first time, he wasn't chasing glory alone—he was chasing a future with Jada, and he refused to let old mistakes tear them apart again.

CHAPTER TWENTY-EIGHT

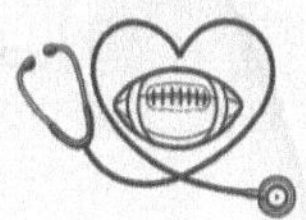

*J*ada stepped onto the worn turf, clutching a small duffel of therapy gear. Her heart tugged at a memory: years ago, she'd rushed across this same field to congratulate Hakeem after a triumphant home game. Back then, it had been all excitement and promise. Now, a cautious new hope mingled with a quiet sense of dread.

Hakeem was already there, kneeling at the fifty-yard line, knee brace visible beneath running shorts. He adjusted his shoelaces, jaw set in determination. A wave of tenderness washed over her—*he's giving this another shot, but for the right reasons.*

She approached slowly, the sun dipping low behind the bleachers, casting the field in a warm, orange glow. "Ready for your big test run?" she asked lightly.

He looked up with a small, crooked smile. "As ready as I can be. My knee's a little tight from the farm this morning, but I'll manage." He stood, wincing a bit before straightening to his full height.

Jada frowned slightly, setting down her duffel. "We can stretch you out first. Don't push too far."

"I won't," he promised. His voice held the familiar mix of excitement and caution. "But if I'm going to that workout in Houston, I need to see if I can do basic drills—cuts, pivots, maybe some short sprints."

She nodded, retrieving a roll of athletic tape from the duffel. "Let me tape your knee for extra stability." She knelt, carefully peeling strips of tape while he braced a hand on her shoulder for balance. The familiarity of tending to his injuries—once a teenage dream for her as an aspiring PT—sparked an odd, nostalgic ache.

"There," she said, smoothing the final piece of tape. "How's that feel?"

He tested a short bend, exhaling. "Better. You always did have a knack for this."

A tiny smile curved her lips. "That's why I made it my career." Rising to her feet, she dusted off her knees. "All right, let's do some dynamic warmups. High knees, butt kicks, maybe a few lunges."

His warm gaze flickered with gratitude, but he merely nodded, beginning the drills with methodical effort. She positioned herself to watch his form, noting each time his brace hissed softly or his foot placement staggered. Her chest tightened whenever he grimaced, even slightly. "Don't force range if it hurts," she warned, heart pounding.

After a few sets, he paused, rubbing his kneecap. "It's okay," he murmured. "Just stiff."

She walked over, placing a gentle hand on his forearm. "You sure you want to do sprints today? We can scale back."

He straightened, a flicker of resolve crossing his features. "I need to try at least a few. If it's too much, I'll stop."

Her stomach knotted, but she forced a supportive nod. "Okay. Let's do it."

They lined up at the goal line. The air hung thick with dusk's humidity, the sweet smell of cut grass stirring old memories of high school games and pep rallies. *This is where it all began for us,* she thought, heart twinging.

Hakeem flexed his leg, took a measured breath, then pushed off in a short sprint down the field. Jada's pulse thudded as she watched him pick up speed. At about fifteen yards, he slowed, limping just slightly. Her concern flared.

Jogging over, she touched his shoulder. "You okay?"

He held up a hand, catching his breath. "Yeah. Knee twinged, but not sharp pain. Just… reminding me it's not fully back yet."

She studied him. "If it's more than a twinge, we stop."

He hesitated, gaze drifting to the distant scoreboard. "Let me try a lateral drill. If I can handle cutting side to side, that'll tell me a lot."

Despite her worry, she nodded. *He has to see for himself.*

They set up a line of cones—borrowed from the rec center—spaced a few yards apart. She stood at one end while he crouched at the start, poised like he was back in the final days of high school practice. A flicker of that confident grin tugged his mouth, though uncertainty lingered in his eyes.

On her signal, he darted between cones in a zigzag. Each pivot made her heart clench, but he stayed balanced, his brace supporting the knee. He did three reps before coming to an abrupt stop, hands braced on his thighs, chest heaving.

"That's…pretty good," she said softly, stepping closer. "How's the pain?"

He grimaced, wiping sweat from his brow. "It's manageable. But I feel how different it is—less explosive."

She pressed a hand to his shoulder. "That could improve with more consistent therapy. You've come a long way already."

He nodded, though his jaw tightened with pent-up frustration. "But is it enough for an NFL-level workout?" The question carried a quiet desperation.

Jada's chest tightened, recalling all the nights he must've dreamed of a triumphant comeback. "We still have two weeks," she reminded him gently. "We can ramp up your regimen. But you have to listen to your body. Don't chase an illusion."

He exhaled slowly. "You're right. I'm—just anxious. I want clarity, you know? Either I can do this or I can't."

"Clarity takes time," she murmured, letting her hand slide down to interlace fingers with his. The small gesture felt both comforting and intimate. "That's why we practice…together."

His gaze softened. "Thanks, Jada."

As they walked back to the goal line, a breeze rustled the bleachers, carrying faint echoes of old cheers. Hakeem stilled, eyes drifting over the empty seats. "Feels surreal being out here. Like I never left, and yet everything's different."

She squeezed his hand. "We're different."

He turned to her, expression raw. "I don't regret where we are now, no matter how this ends."

Warmth flooded her chest, tears pricking the edge of her vision. "Me neither," she whispered, heart twisting at the sincerity in his voice.

They wrapped up the session with light cooldown stretches, and then she carefully peeled off the athletic tape. She could see faint redness where the brace rubbed. His kneecap seemed slightly swollen—mild, but enough to remind her this was still a fragile recovery.

"Let's ice it tonight," she said, worry creeping in. "I can help if you want. Or… maybe you're tired of me bossing you around."

A low chuckle escaped him. "I'll never get tired of you." Then, quieter, "An ice session together sounds good."

BY THE TIME they gathered the cones and gear, twilight had settled over the field. The scoreboard's dark outline loomed against the purple sky. Jada stood by her car, gaze roaming the silent stands. She couldn't shake the wistful swirl of memories: cheer routines, post-game hugs, the star quarterback who'd owned her heart.

Hakeem drew close, placing a gentle hand on her waist. "Penny for your thoughts?"

She leaned against the car, letting the memory-laden silence sit between them. "Just… remembering high school. We were so sure of everything back then. College, the NFL, us…like it was all guaranteed."

His face tightened with regret. "I messed that up."

She touched his cheek lightly. "We both changed, Hakeem. Don't carry it alone."

A moment passed, the hum of cicadas in the distance. Then he pressed a soft kiss to her forehead, the gesture so tender it made her ache with a fierce kind of love. "Ready to head out?" he asked, voice husky.

She nodded, stepping back. "Yeah. Let's get ice on that knee."

They parted ways, each driving to his home—her trunk loaded with therapy gear, her mind laden with cautious hope. He'd do the workout, or maybe he wouldn't. She just knew that for the first time, they were facing it side by side. *No more secrets, no more heartbreak alone.*

As she watched his taillights disappear down the road, a quiet conviction settled over her. Whatever lay ahead—NFL or Sweetgum Meadows or some middle ground—she'd stand with him, every painful pivot and hopeful stride, believing that this time, they'd find the path that kept them together.

CHAPTER TWENTY-NINE

Jada shifted on her office chair, glancing for the third time at the clock on the wall. *He should be here any minute.* She reached for Hakeem's file, flipping through the notes about his knee exercises and incremental improvements. A faint smile tugged her lips—*He's really worked hard.*

Yet a simmering nervousness pooled in her chest. Ever since their practice on the high school field, Hakeem had dedicated himself to a stricter rehab schedule, determined to gauge his readiness. If today's checkup with Dr. Hayes went well, he'd officially schedule the workout in Houston. *That means we're one step closer to him actually leaving,* she reminded herself, a pang of worry threading through her mind.

Soft footsteps in the hallway made her look up. A moment later, Hakeem appeared in the doorway, wearing athletic shorts and a loose hoodie. His expression brightened when he saw her, though tension lined his brow.

"Hey, Doc," he said, voice gentle. "You look busy."

She offered a small grin. "Busy day, but I'm never too busy

for a certain stubborn patient." Setting aside her laptop, she rose. "You ready for Dr. Hayes?"

"As ready as I can be," he replied, mouth twisting in a grimace. "I just hope he doesn't say I'm insane to try."

Jada's heart squeezed with sympathy. Stepping around her desk, she brushed a hand along his elbow in a quick gesture of reassurance. "We'll see what he says. You've done everything right—kept up with therapy, balanced rest and exercise. Let's trust the process."

He nodded, exhaling. "Thanks, Jada."

They walked down the corridor together, passing familiar faces who offered cheerful waves or knowing smiles. *Word of the NFL possibility must be circling,* Jada thought. She caught a glimpse of Inez, the friendly nurse, giving Hakeem a thumbs-up as though to say "You've got this."

At the end of the hallway, Dr. Hayes' office loomed. A nurse ushered them into the exam room. Jada noticed how Hakeem's shoulders tensed, like an athlete waiting for the final whistle. She gave his hand a discreet squeeze before letting go. *We'll face this together.*

Dr. Hayes entered with a quick, professional stride. "Hakeem, good to see you again." He offered a polite nod to Jada. "Dr. Davis, I hear you've been handling his physical therapy?"

Jada kept her tone brisk, professional. "Yes, sir. He's made considerable progress in range of motion and strength. Minimal swelling after moderate activity. We're here to see if he's cleared for a higher level of exertion."

Dr. Hayes adjusted his glasses, consulting a tablet. "That's what I gather. Let's check your knee, do some tests, see where we stand."

Hakeem hopped onto the exam table, wincing slightly at the brace's position. Jada stood by, arms folded, eyes sharp on every movement. Dr. Hayes ran Hakeem through a series of tests—

flexion, extension, lateral stability. Each time Hakeem moved, Jada watched for any flicker of pain that might undermine his confidence.

"How's it feel?" Dr. Hayes asked, pressing gently around the patella.

Hakeem exhaled through his nose. "A bit sore, but not debilitating. Definitely stronger than a month ago."

"Good," Dr. Hayes said. He stepped back, peering at his notes. "Based on your progress and imaging, I'd say you're close to being game-ready—assuming you continue a disciplined regimen and don't over-train too soon. NFL is intense. You'll need absolute caution in those first high-impact drills."

A rush of relief and fear rippled through Jada. *He's basically cleared.* She darted a glance at Hakeem, whose shoulders slumped in a mix of excitement and nerves.

"So you think it's possible?" Hakeem asked, voice tight.

The doctor nodded. "Yes, it's possible. You're not at one hundred percent, but if a team's willing to work with your continued therapy, you could rejoin the league. Of course, there's always risk. Re-injury could be worse. But physically, you've recovered well."

Hakeem let out a breath. "Thank you, sir."

Dr. Hayes tapped his tablet with a stylus. "I'll email you guidelines, and you should keep Dr. Davis or another PT in the loop if you travel for workouts. Don't skip sessions. Understood?"

"Yes, absolutely," Hakeem said, glancing at Jada. "We're on the same page."

She forced a smile, heart thumping. *We're doing this. He's cleared. He can go.*

Dr. Hayes nodded his approval, made a few final notes, then left them with a short congratulation. The second the door closed, the exam room felt smaller, the tension pressing on Jada's chest.

"So… that's it," she breathed, trying for steady calm. "You're officially good to attempt the Houston tryout."

Hakeem slid off the table, leaning on the brace momentarily. "Yeah. Guess I should call the Fury rep and set up a date." His eyes flicked to hers. "But only if you're still okay with it."

A quiet ache flared in her. *If she said no, would he stay?* The thought twisted her stomach. She swallowed, stepping closer. "I promised I wouldn't hold you back. If you need to do this, then do it."

He studied her face, fingers brushing hers gently. "Then we'll do it. Together. If it doesn't feel right, I'm done. If it does…we figure out a plan that keeps us both happy."

Her throat tightened at the intensity in his eyes. "I'm trying so hard not to be scared," she admitted in a hushed tone.

His grip on her hand firmed. "I know. And I'm terrified too —of hurting you again." He paused, exhaling. "Let's take it one step at a time, yeah?"

She nodded, a shaky smile curving her lips. *One step at a time.*

They left the exam room side by side, the quiet hallway amplifying the storm of emotions swirling within her. She flashed a nod at Dr. Hayes through the glass partition, gratitude and uncertainty warring in her gut. *In a few weeks, he'll be in Houston. Then what?*

THEY DECIDED to grab a quick bite at Rochelle's Old-Fashioned Diner. They slid into a booth near the window, ordering burgers and fries more out of habit than hunger.

Malachi wandered over with a knowing grin. "Hey, you two. Heard the good news that Hakeem's knee is basically cleared?"

Jada's stomach twisted—*How does everyone find out so fast?*— but she managed a polite nod. "Yeah, Dr. Hayes says he's good to go for a workout."

"Nice," Malachi said, beaming. "Man, I remember seeing you in your final high school game. You had that unstoppable drive." He gave Hakeem a playful punch on the shoulder. "If you end up back in the league, I'll brag that you used to eat here all the time."

Hakeem laughed lightly, though tension shadowed his eyes. "We'll see, man. One day at a time."

Malachi nodded sagely. "Totally. Anyway, your food'll be out soon. On the house if you make it big again." He winked, then bustled off.

Jada let out a breath, leaning her elbows on the table. "I keep forgetting how excited people get around here."

Hakeem's gaze swept over the half-full diner, where a couple of older women were openly watching them. "I know. Makes me feel grateful and guilty all at once." He hesitated, voice softening. "You sure you're okay?"

She studied him—a man who once left to chase a dream, now possibly doing it again, but with heartbreak in his rearview mirror. *If I ask him to stay, would he resent me? If I encourage him to go, will I resent him if he leaves?*

She forced a small nod. "Yes. Just…nervous. But I trust you."

His features lit with relief, and he gently covered her hands with his own. "Thank you," he said, voice hushed. "I won't betray that trust."

Malachi reappeared, sliding plates of burgers and fries onto the table. "Here you go, enjoy," he said, bounding off again.

They attempted a light conversation, nibbling fries and sipping soda, but the looming trip to Houston hung over them. She found herself repeating a mental mantra: *One step at a time.* When they finished, they paid and stepped into the warm Sweetgum evening, streetlamps flickering on.

Hakeem walked her to her car, the hush of Main Street wrapping around them. She turned to him, heart pounding with all the unresolved fears. "You'll call them tomorrow?"

He nodded. "Yeah. Likely schedule the workout for sometime next week."

She inhaled, summoning courage. "Then… let me help you with final drills. We'll go over agility again, maybe do a few passing routines if you want to gauge your throwing stance with that knee."

A flicker of longing passed through his eyes, for a moment reminiscent of that star quarterback she'd known as a teen. "I'd love that," he murmured, voice catching. "You helping me train… it's like coming full circle."

She swallowed, tears threatening. "I just want you safe and happy—whatever that ends up meaning."

His smile trembled. He swept her into a gentle hug, arms strong around her. She let out a shaky breath against his chest, listening to the steady thump of his heartbeat. *I can be brave if he's brave too.*

"Thank you, Jada," he whispered, pressing a light kiss to her temple. "We'll figure this out."

She nodded, exhaling into the warmth of his shirt. "We will."

Stepping back, she slipped into her car, reluctantly letting his hand go. As she drove away, she watched him in the rearview mirror—a solitary figure on the sidewalk, knee brace still visible, gaze following her until she turned the corner.

Clenching the wheel, she felt a subtle ache bloom within her. *In a week's time, he'd stand on a professional field again. Would it be everything he remembered—or would it tear them apart all over?* The unknown gnawed at her, but she forced herself to trust in their hard-won communication and the love that had brought them back together.

For now, that trust—and each other—would have to be enough.

CHAPTER THIRTY

The echo of his footsteps bounced off the polished floor as Hakeem made his way down the corridor of the Houston Fury's training facility. In his right hand, he clutched a small duffel bag with workout clothes, a spare knee brace, and a sense of resolve that wavered between excitement and dread. The facility hummed with activity—voices calling out drills, weights clanging in a nearby gym, the scent of fresh turf permeating the air.

He paused at a glass door labeled Locker Room B, inhaling to steady his heart rate. *You've done this a thousand times.* But never quite like this—carrying the knowledge that if he succeeded, he'd be facing the NFL all over again… and risking the life he'd started rebuilding in Sweetgum with Jada.

His phone buzzed in his pocket. He fished it out, relief flooding him at the sight of Jada's name on the screen:

> You've got this. 🤍 Trust your knee. Trust yourself. And text me the second you finish!

A small, shaky smile curved his lips. He sent a quick reply—

Will do, doc. Thanks for believing in me.

—then slid the phone into his bag. *One step at a time, Brown.*

Pushing the locker room door open, he scanned the space: rows of polished metal lockers, bright fluorescent lights. A staffer waved him over, handing him a Fury T-shirt and a small pass with his name on it. "Coach'll call you out onto the field in about fifteen," the staffer explained. "You can warm up here or in the side gym. Need anything?"

Hakeem shook his head. "No, I'm good, thanks."

He found an empty section of the bench, changed into athletic gear, and carefully adjusted his knee brace. The old adrenaline thrummed in his veins, reminiscent of college game days. *It's been so long since I felt this rush.* Another wave of doubt flickered—*What if my knee gives out?* But Jada's voice echoed in his mind: *Trust yourself.*

He forced a measured exhale, rolling his shoulders. Then, with determination, he headed back out into the corridor, following signs to the indoor practice field. Voices rose, echoing off high ceilings. As he stepped through the final set of doors, the brilliant artificial lights revealed a pristine stretch of turf, markers set up for drills, and a handful of Fury staff milling around.

"Hakeem Brown?" called a stern-looking man in a Fury polo. "We're ready for you."

Hakeem nodded, swallowing past the lump in his throat. *Here we go.*

THEY ASKED him to start with basic warm-ups: jogging laps, knee lifts, side-to-side shuffles. Each motion brought a twinge of memory—how he used to power through these drills without a second thought. Now he tracked every signal from his knee, conscious of any stiffness or pain. *Don't overdo it. Jada'll kill me if I do.*

Gradually, they moved to more intense exercises. One of the assistant coaches tossed him a football. "Show us some short passes, see how you plant your feet."

Hakeem took a measured stance, inhaled deeply, and launched the ball to a waiting receiver, who sprinted a crisp route. The throw landed smoothly in the receiver's hands, and a flicker of pride sparked in Hakeem's chest. *Still got it.*

They repeated the sequence, adjusting for longer passes. Hakeem's heart hammered as he felt the old rhythm flow through him—dropping back, scanning a hypothetical defense, firing the ball. Yet each pivot hammered a reminder into his knee: *Not as smooth as it was.*

After the passing drills, the coaches set up cone routes to test his mobility. Sweat trickled down his temple, and the brace hissed with each sharp cut. Pain flared once or twice, but he fought through, mindful not to push too far. Still, the staff eyed him with interest, scribbling notes.

Finally, they waved him over to a water station, letting him catch his breath. The man in the Fury polo—apparently a scouting assistant—met him with a firm nod. "You're showing decent agility, Brown. Still a bit hesitant on that knee?"

Hakeem panted, hands on his hips. "Yeah, some lingering tightness. It's not perfect. But it's miles better than it was."

The man grunted thoughtfully, eyeing the staffers behind him. "We'll do a final round of throws—long passes, if you're up to it. Then we can talk."

Hakeem's pulse jolted. *Long passes... That's where you have to plant the leg firmly.* He closed his eyes, recalling Jada's instructions. *Don't jam your knee, remember your form.* He exhaled. "Let's do it."

~

A HUSH FELL across the practice field as Hakeem lined up. He flexed the knee subtly, the brace digging into his skin. *No fear, Brown. You either can or you can't.*

The assistant coach snapped his fingers, indicating the route: a deep post. The receiver took off, sprinting downfield. Hakeem dropped back, ignoring the phantom feeling of a defensive line that wasn't actually there. He planted the leg, pivoted, launched the ball with every ounce of power he could muster.

Pain rippled at the joint, but the throw soared downfield, spiraling with near-perfect precision. The receiver caught it at the twenty-yard line, a smooth, graceful connection that made one of the coaches let out a low whistle.

Hakeem winced as he straightened, rubbing his knee. The ache was sharper now, but not debilitating. *One more?*

They repeated two more long passes—both decent, though his final pivot nearly buckled him, sending a hot stab of warning through his knee. The staffers gestured him to stop before he overdid it, and he limped over, sweat drenching his shirt.

"Good job, Brown," the scout said, handing him a towel. "We see the potential. Need to discuss with our head coach, GM, medical staff, all that. But… I won't lie. I'm impressed."

Hakeem dabbed his face, every breath rattling in his lungs. "Thanks," he managed, heart pounding from exertion and relief. *It's over. I did it.*

The assistant clapped him on the shoulder. "You'll hear from us within a week. Meantime, keep rehabbing. Don't blow that knee out on a pick-up game or something."

A shaky laugh escaped him. "I won't."

AFTER A QUICK SHOWER in the facility's locker room, Hakeem found himself perched on a bench, phone in hand. Adrenaline still pulsed in his veins, but the dull throb in his knee wouldn't let him forget he wasn't at a hundred percent.

He opened his messages, ignoring the swirl of nerves, and tapped on Jada's name:

> Workout done. Knee held up…ish. Will call you soon.

He stared at the screen, a rush of longing hollowing his chest. *Wish she could've been here.* But the hospital needed her, and in truth, he'd wanted to prove to himself he could face this alone. Maybe he was still that star quarterback—*maybe.*

His phone buzzed almost instantly:

> ISH? That's not reassuring. You OK? Call me, please!

A weary grin tugged his lips. He tapped the phone icon and lifted it to his ear. She picked up on the first ring.

"You worried me," she accused lightly, though he heard the tremor of genuine concern. "Are you hurt?"

"Not badly," he murmured, leaning against the cool metal of the locker. "Got some knee pain, but I managed. I…did okay, I think."

A slow exhale echoed through the line. "Thank goodness. Did they give you any feedback?"

He closed his eyes. "They said they were impressed. They'll talk to the head coach and GM. I'll hear back in a week, apparently."

"That's great." Relief and tension mingled in her voice. "So… how do you feel?"

He tried to parse his jumbled emotions. "Proud? Worried I can't handle a full season? Glad I tried? All of that, plus I miss you." His throat tightened. "Wish you were here."

"I miss you too," she admitted softly. "Any chance you can head home tonight?"

He glanced at the time, noting the flights. "Yeah, I'll catch the next flight back. Should land in the evening."

"Good," she breathed. "I'll pick you up at the airport."

A wave of gratitude washed over him. "Thanks, Jada. I… owe you everything."

She gave a quiet laugh. "You owe me a pain report on that knee, and maybe a promise you'll keep icing it."

He smiled, a knot in his chest easing. "Deal."

They lingered a moment longer, exchanging soft reassurances, before hanging up. Rising, Hakeem slipped the phone into his bag, aware that the next days would be a waiting game. But he felt lighter, bolstered by Jada's unwavering support.

Gathering his things, he made his way out of the facility. A few staffers bid him farewell with polite nods. The Houston sun blazed as he stepped outside, but all he could think of was the drive to the airport—and then home, to Sweetgum and Jada's arms.

Regardless of what the Fury decided, one truth remained: *He'd never let a dream overshadow what truly mattered—her.*

CHAPTER THIRTY-ONE

The terminal doors slid open, releasing a modest crowd of disembarking passengers into the small lobby. Jada stood on tiptoes, scanning over heads until she caught sight of Hakeem's broad shoulders and distinctive brace peeking beneath loose jeans. Her heart thudded at the mixture of exhaustion and relief in his eyes.

She waved, stepping away from the roped-off waiting area. His gaze locked onto her, and a soft, grateful smile curved his lips. A rush of warmth shot through her chest—*He's back.*

"How was the flight?" she asked, voice quiet as he approached.

He set down his carry-on bag, exhaling. "Long," he admitted, arms encircling her in a gentle hug. The tension in his muscles was palpable, bearing witness to the physically and emotionally draining day. "Glad to be here."

She let herself sink into his warmth for a moment, the hum of the small airport fading to the background. "I'm glad too."

He pulled back, brushing a thumb over her cheek. "My knee's stiff, but I survived. Let's get out of here."

Nodding, she lifted the strap of his duffel onto her shoulder. "Deal."

As Jada navigated the winding roads back toward town, the sky glowed with the last streaks of orange. Hakeem leaned back in the passenger seat, eyes drifting over the familiar pastures and distant tree lines.

"So," she ventured, gripping the wheel. "Got any more details? They'll let you know in a week?"

He rubbed his knee absently. "Yeah. They seemed positive, but you never know. Coach has to watch the footage, consult the medical staff. A lot could change." His voice stayed even, though the taut line of his jaw betrayed his anxiety.

Jada kept her gaze on the road, heart squeezing. "And… how do you feel about it now that it's done?"

A pause hung between them. Finally, he answered, voice lower. "Relieved I did it. Proud I could still throw, even if it hurt. But I couldn't ignore how much weaker my knee was. Part of me wonders if I'm forcing something that's not meant to be."

Her chest tightened with empathy. "You did all you could. That's what matters."

He cast her a sideways glance, something warm in his eyes. "Jada, I wouldn't have even gotten this far without you."

A shy smile tugged her lips. "I just handed you some exercise sheets and taped your knee."

He scoffed, gently resting his hand on hers atop the gearshift. "No. You believed in me, even when I didn't. You gave me reason to come back if this all fell apart."

She squeezed his hand, a lump forming in her throat. *No matter what happens, we're facing it together.* "Then let's see what the Fury decides."

He nodded, eyes turning back to the twilight-soaked countryside. "Yeah. One day at a time."

They arrived at Jada's apartment complex just as dusk settled into the purple haze of night. Dim lights from the small parking lot illuminated the path. She watched Hakeem climb out, wincing slightly as his brace caught on the car door. Her PT instincts flared.

"How bad is the pain?" she asked, slinging his duffel over her shoulder again.

He ran a hand over the brace, wincing. "A five out of ten, maybe. Could be worse."

She arched a brow. "I'll get ice on that. Come inside?"

He smiled wearily. "If you're offering, I'd love to crash here tonight. But only if it's okay."

A flutter of contentment bloomed in her chest. "It's more than okay."

They headed up the narrow staircase to her studio. A few neighbors' doors were cracked open, music drifting faintly. Inside her apartment, she flicked on the lamp, warm light spilling over the small couch and kitchenette.

"Sit," she ordered softly, directing him to the couch. "I'll grab ice."

He complied, sinking onto the cushions with a hiss of breath. She ducked into her freezer, retrieving an ice pack and a towel. Returning, she gently eased his brace off, mindful of each strap. "Lean back."

The hush of the evening wrapped around them as she positioned the pack over his knee. He let out a quiet groan of relief. "Feels good."

She settled beside him, heart heavy with the knowledge of how uncertain everything remained. "So... we wait."

He nodded, gaze flickering to her with tired gratitude. "Yeah, we wait." His eyes held a question she understood: *Are you still with me, even if the league calls?*

She covered his hand, giving a reassuring squeeze. "We knew this would be the hardest part—waiting, not knowing."

He exhaled, tension melting from his shoulders. "At least I'm home. I hated not having you there for moral support."

She leaned her head on his shoulder. "Well, I'm here now."

They sat in silence, listening to the soft hum of her fridge and the distant traffic on Main Street. Eventually, she rose to fetch him water, rummaging for some ibuprofen. He accepted both with a murmured thanks, swallowing the pills.

She perched beside him again, letting him rest his head against the couch. His eyes slipped shut, exhaustion carving lines into his face. Gently, she stroked his hair, remembering their teenage days when he'd collapse on her porch swing post-game, half-asleep while she chattered about stats.

"Stay here," she whispered, half to herself, half to him. "No matter what happens."

He cracked open an eye, voice rough. "That's the plan."

Warmth suffused her, something akin to peace settling in her bones. Whether the NFL said yes or no, Hakeem was here— choosing *her*, choosing Sweetgum, or at least vowing not to repeat past mistakes. *We'll cross the next bridge when it comes.*

As hours slipped by, the ice pack melted, and she refreshed it once. The hush grew deeper, the only glow a single lamp casting gold across his face. They talked in low voices about random things: stories from his Houston trip, her day at the hospital, the silly rumors swirling about them in town. Laughter bubbled up every so often, like a balm against the tension.

When midnight neared, she rose, nudging him gently. "Come on, you can't sleep on the couch in that position. Let's get you stretched out."

He blinked, surfacing from a doze. "Sorry. Didn't mean to crash."

She smirked, helping him stand. "Don't apologize for being tired after a big day. You want the bed? I can take the couch."

He frowned. "Not a chance. If you're comfortable…sharing again, I'd like that."

Her pulse fluttered, memories of nights they'd spent

wrapped in each other's arms. She exhaled, letting the lingering fear slip away. "Yes. I'd like that too."

They moved to her small bedroom area, separated by a partial wall. She helped him unstrap the brace fully, gently massaging the area around his knee with practiced motions. He hissed occasionally but gave her a grateful look.

"Sorry if I'm being bossy," she whispered, pressing her thumb to a tight muscle.

A small laugh escaped him. "I like bossy when it's you." Then, softly, "Thank you."

She finished, heart humming with quiet affection. "All done. Let's get some rest."

He gingerly slid onto the bed, and she joined him, switching off the lamp. In the dark, he curled an arm around her waist, and she snuggled close, his warmth a comfort against the unknown future. *He's home, at least for tonight.*

"Jada?" he murmured in the darkness.

"Hm?" She pressed her cheek to his shoulder.

"I'm...scared," he admitted, voice hushed. "Scared they'll want me and I'll have to decide. Scared they won't want me and I'll feel like I failed. Scared you'll think I'm not worthy either way."

Her heart clenched. She let out a soft sigh, tightening her hold on him. "Hakeem, you're worthy—NFL or not. If they pass, we figure something else out. If they want you, we decide *together*. I won't let you face that alone."

He breathed a trembling breath, brushing his lips to her temple. "Thank you," he repeated, voice cracking.

She closed her eyes, letting the steady beat of his heart lull her. *We'll get through this.* The looming decision hung in the corners of her mind, but for now, they embraced in the protective cocoon of midnight, forging a trust she prayed would weather whatever news came next.

As sleep claimed her, she thought only of how solid he felt beside her—and how, even if the world demanded more from him, she'd be right here, holding on.

CHAPTER THIRTY-TWO

A gentle breeze rustled the potted plants on Jada's small windowsill. She stood at her kitchenette, absentmindedly stirring sugar into her morning coffee. Sleep had been sporadic lately—too many nights spent listening to Hakeem's deep breathing, wondering if they'd soon face another goodbye. *He's here now*, she reminded herself, but the question of the NFL hovered like a stubborn cloud.

In the other corner of her studio, Hakeem scrolled through his phone, a frown creasing his brow. The brace lay on the floor beside him, evidence of how he'd started giving it a break now that he was mostly off his feet. Each beep or buzz from his phone felt loaded with possibility.

She cleared her throat, walking over to hand him a mug of coffee. "No word yet?"

He exhaled, brushing a hand across his stubble. "Nothing new. Just random social media stuff." His eyes flicked up, gratitude warming his gaze. "Thanks for the coffee."

She nodded, settling on the couch. "They said a week, right?"

He joined her, shoulders sagging. "Yeah. Feels longer."

Setting his phone aside, he rubbed at his knee absently. "At least it's not hurting too much."

She placed a calming hand over his. "That's something. Dr. Hayes' guidelines still hold—no overexertion, but normal movement. We can keep therapy sessions at the hospital, or I can do them here if you prefer."

A faint smile touched his lips. "You, playing in-home therapist? Careful, I might get used to that."

She rolled her eyes, fighting a smile of her own. "I still have *other* patients, you know."

"And I still have a bag of frozen peas with my name on it," he teased back, though a flicker of tension remained beneath the light banter.

Just then, Jada's phone buzzed on the kitchen counter. She stood, checking the screen: a text from her mother, likely about the weekend family dinner. She typed a quick reply—

Yes, we'll come. No, we can't confirm the NFL thing yet.

She stifled a laugh at how Mom's curiosity flared weekly. *Everyone in town is on pins and needles.*

"Your mom?" Hakeem guessed.

"Yep," she said, sliding the phone into her pocket. "They want us over for dinner Sunday. I said yes, if you're up for it."

He exhaled softly. "Sure, let's do it. If we haven't heard from Houston by then, we can at least enjoy a normal evening."

A twist of affection mingled with sorrow in her heart. *He's bracing for a yes or no.* "We'll survive either way, you know," she said gently, resting a hand on his shoulder.

He placed his hand over hers, voice low. "I'm trying to believe that."

∾

Despite Rochelle's retirement, the diner remained the pulse of local gossip. Jada had suggested they grab lunch there, hoping a short change of scenery might distract Hakeem from the silent phone.

They slid into a booth near the window. Malachi bustled over, dishing out water glasses and an easy grin. "Hey, you two." He hesitated, glancing at Hakeem's phone. "Any news?"

Hakeem forced a smile. "Not yet."

Malachi gave an understanding nod. "Well, we're all rooting for you. But you know that."

Jada's chest fluttered. *Rooting for him—but also for them.* She gave Malachi a polite smile, then studied the menu though she nearly had it memorized. *Better to feign busyness than dwell on the wait.*

A couple booths away, Mrs. Andrews and Mrs. Bridges huddled together, occasionally shooting covert glances in their direction. Jada caught snatches of conversation—something about "the big leagues." She sighed inwardly. *Town rumor mill is in full force.*

Hakeem must've noticed too, because he lowered his voice. "Think I should stand up and announce, 'No word yet, folks'?"

A wry laugh escaped her. "Might save them the trouble of eavesdropping."

He leaned back, fiddling with his water glass. "I guess it's kind of sweet how they care."

She patted his hand. "That's Sweetgum for you."

They returned to Jada's apartment, taking a short stroll around the block first to let Hakeem's knee move naturally. Each step brought a mild stiffness, but no real pain. Jada silently thanked every therapy session that led him here— functional, hopeful, yet perched on the edge of a major decision.

She opened her door, ushering him inside. The studio felt warm, faintly sunlit. Turning to him, she mustered a soft smile.

CHAPTER THIRTY-TWO

"Want me to whip up something for dinner? Or we can order in."

He set his phone on the coffee table, tapping the screen to check for missed calls. Nothing. "Takeout might be easier," he said, dropping onto the couch. "I don't have the energy to pretend to enjoy cooking right now."

Her heart twisted with compassion. "Takeout it is. Burgers or Chinese?"

He shrugged. "Chinese, maybe? I know Mrs. Zhang always packs extra dumplings if I'm the one picking up."

Jada was about to answer when his phone abruptly vibrated, skittering across the table. They froze, exchanging wide-eyed looks. *Houston calling?*

Hakeem snatched it up, breath catching. "It's an unknown number."

Her stomach flipped, and she eased beside him, heart in her throat. "Answer," she urged, adrenaline hitting her veins.

He pressed the screen. "Hello?" His voice came out a bit rough.

She watched every flicker of his expression—first surprise, then caution, then a guarded neutrality. She strained to hear the words on the other end but only caught a muffled male voice. Hakeem nodded a few times, a fleeting smile stirring but vanishing quickly.

"Yes, sir," he said. "I understand." Another pause, his jaw tightening. "Thanks for the update. I appreciate it."

The call ended, leaving a tense hush. Hakeem slowly set the phone down, gaze fixed on the device as though it might bite him. Her heart pounded. *What's the verdict?*

"Well?" she asked softly, resisting the urge to grab his hand.

He let out a long breath. "They, uh…like my arm, but they're worried about my knee's longevity," he said, voice thick. "They're inviting me to training camp on a conditional basis— like a short-term contract if I can prove I'm stable enough."

A swirl of relief, dread, and confusion filled her chest. "So… that means they want you, but they're not guaranteeing anything?"

He nodded, running a hand over his face. "Basically. I'd have to move to Houston for camp, work out with the team. If the knee holds up, I can earn a roster spot. If not, I'm out."

She swallowed, trying to keep her voice steady. "I see. And… do they need an answer right away?"

"In the next couple days," he murmured. "Camp starts soon."

A heavy silence weighed on them. *Days.* That was all the time they had to decide their future. She fought a surge of panic —*He might be gone for months, or forever.*

Finally, Hakeem lifted his eyes, raw turmoil shining there. "I don't know what to do, Jada," he confessed, voice trembling. "Part of me wants to chase it, see if I can still be that guy. But the other part—" His gaze flicked to her, full of longing. "I'm scared I'll lose us if I go."

Her throat stung with tears she refused to shed. She placed a hand on his knee, the warmth of him grounding her. "We talked about this," she whispered, breath unsteady. "You should try if it feels right. I won't vanish. I just—" She swallowed hard. "I don't want to be the reason you always wonder 'What if?'"

He squeezed his eyes shut. "I never wanted to put you in this position again."

She forced a tremulous smile, tears burning. "We're here now. Let's figure it out. If you go, I'll— I'll support you from here. And if it looks like you're healthy enough, maybe we find a way for me to visit?" Her heart clenched at the idea of uprooting her entire life, but she refused to block him. "We'll communicate, do weekly check-ins?"

His gaze shimmered with emotion. "You'd do that?"

A tear slipped free, and she brushed it away quickly. "Of course, Hakeem. I love you, and I want you to be sure of your path."

He let out a quiet sob of relief, pulling her into a fierce hug. She clung to him, burying her face in the crook of his neck. *We're going to face this. We have no choice.*

They remained there, wrapped in each other, the phone on the table a silent reminder of how quickly life could change. She felt his heart pounding against her, both of them trembling with the weight of the decision. If he left for camp, would their fragile second chance survive?

She inhaled, summoning a calm she wasn't sure she possessed. "We'll get through it," she whispered, though fear prickled her skin. "One day at a time. Right?"

"Right," he murmured, voice choked. "One day at a time."

And as the last vestiges of daylight slipped through the window, they held onto each other like lifelines, knowing that the road ahead might separate them physically, but determined to keep the bond they'd rebuilt strong—no matter how far apart the NFL might drag him from Sweetgum.

CHAPTER THIRTY-THREE

The morning sunlight filtered through the blinds of Jada's apartment, illuminating the modest living space in a gentle glow. Hakeem stood by the window, phone in hand, staring at the newly arrived email from the Houston Fury. He could barely process the swirl of text on the screen: reporting dates, training camp schedules, a short-term contract contingent on a final medical check once he arrived. *They really want me to do this,* he thought.

Across the room, Jada sat at her small dining table, flipping through a folded set of therapy notes—likely reviewing his final at-home regimen. She glanced up, meeting his eyes. He offered her a faint nod, something akin to *It's official* lingering in the air.

She must've read the gravity on his face. Setting aside the papers, she motioned for him to join her. "Tell me everything," she said softly, voice carrying a mixture of steadiness and sorrow.

He crossed the room, taking the chair across from her. "They need me in Houston next week. If I pass their physical, I'll start training camp right away. It's a short-term deal, but if my knee holds up, it could become a full contract."

Her lips pressed together. "That's… fast."

"Yeah." He raked a hand over his hair, tension coiled in his muscles. "I was hoping for a bit more time. But I guess the league doesn't wait around."

A hush settled, broken only by the hum of Jada's air conditioner. He recalled the vow they'd made: *No big decisions without each other.* Taking her hand, he forced himself to be transparent. "I don't want to upend us again. But—"

She squeezed his hand. "But you feel like you have to try, or you'll always wonder," she finished gently. At his solemn nod, she inhaled. "Okay. Then let's figure out how to make it work."

Emotion swelled in his chest, relief mixing with guilt. *She's so selfless, even though I know this hurts her.* "I could get an apartment in Houston temporarily," he ventured. "Focus on training. We do video calls daily, visits when possible." He grimaced at how meager that sounded.

Jada swallowed, shoulders rigid. "We can manage that for a while. Long-distance isn't ideal, but… we've come so far. I won't bail just because it's tough."

His heart ached. "I just hate that I'm leaving so soon, right when we finally started our life together."

She nodded, tears brightening her eyes, though she held them at bay. "Me too. But you're not gone forever, right?" A flicker of forced hope laced her tone. "If your knee says no, you'll come back. If you make the team, we talk about whether I can relocate, or if we split our time. Something."

The weight of that unknown pressed heavily on him. "That's a lot for you."

She shook her head with quiet resolve. "We'll figure it out. I'd rather face it together than let you walk away without trying."

His throat constricted. Leaning over the table, he brushed a soft kiss to her knuckles. "Thank you, Jada. I don't deserve how amazing you are."

She exhaled shakily, blinking back tears. "Just... promise me we'll communicate. No shutting me out. If it's too hard, tell me. If your knee flares up, be honest."

He nodded, sliding his chair closer. "I promise. Same goes for you—if you feel neglected or lonely, call me out."

A tremulous laugh escaped her. "I will."

HAKEEM STOOD in his modest bedroom at the Brown farm, suitcase open on the bed. His older brother, Rashad, lingered by the dresser, arms folded. A swirl of old football jerseys lay piled on the sheets—remnants of a dream he once believed was everything.

"You sure about this?" Rashad asked quietly. "I see how torn you are."

Hakeem zipped a sweatshirt into the suitcase. "I'm not sure," he admitted. "But I can't let fear stop me from finding out if I can still play."

Rashad nodded, expression thoughtful. "And Jada?"

A pang tugged Hakeem's chest. "She's supportive. Scared, but supportive." He paused, scanning the room. "We're trying to do it right this time—no secrets, no running off with zero warning."

Rashad clapped him on the back. "Proud of you, bro. Remember, if it doesn't feel right, you can come home."

The word *home* echoed in Hakeem's mind. Once upon a time, *home* was an NFL stadium. Now, he recognized that *home* was this farm, Jada, and Sweetgum. "Thanks," he whispered.

BEFORE LEAVING FOR HOUSTON, Hakeem insisted on dropping by the hospital to finalize some therapy notes with Jada's department. Officially, he wanted copies of his progress reports for the Fury's medical team. But really, it was an excuse to see her in her professional realm—reminding himself of the life he was momentarily stepping away from.

He found her in a small consultation room, tidying up after a patient. She smiled at his entrance, but her eyes bore a wistful concern. "Hey."

"Hey," he said, voice quiet. "Got the printouts from the front desk. Figured I should say goodbye. Officially."

She set aside a folder, stepping closer. They were alone in the room, the hum of air vents the only background noise. "When's your flight?"

"Tomorrow morning. Early." He held her gaze, heart pounding. "I'll text you from the airport."

She nodded, forcing a small smile. "I'll be waiting." A hush settled, then she reached up to smooth the collar of his shirt. "Please remember everything Dr. Hayes said—don't hide any pain, don't push through if it feels wrong."

He gently enclosed her hand in his. "I promise." Clearing his throat, he let out a shaky breath. "We can do this, right?"

Emotion flickered in her eyes. "We can," she murmured, voice tight with unshed tears. "Just don't forget to call me. Every day if you can."

He pressed his forehead to hers, breathing in the faint scent of sanitizer and coffee that clung to her uniform. "I will. And… I love you."

A tremor passed through her. "I love you too, Hakeem."

For a moment, they indulged in a tender kiss—soft, reassuring, yet brimming with the ache of impending separation. Then she slipped away, blinking quickly. He could see the effort it took for her to stay composed in her workplace. "Go," she said gently, voice shaking. "Pack, rest, be ready to show them what you're made of."

He nodded, jaw clenched. "I will."

They exchanged one last look—one that said *This isn't goodbye forever*—before he forced himself to leave. As the hospital corridors swallowed him, he clenched his fists, each step echoing the vow he kept repeating: *I'm coming back to you, Jada.*

~

JADA INSISTED on driving him halfway, though he'd get a shuttle at a nearby station to the airport the next morning. They traveled in a subdued hush, her hand occasionally slipping over to rest on his knee as he drummed tense fingers on his seat.

"It's just a few weeks," he murmured, as though trying to convince them both.

She offered a watery smile. "Just a few weeks," she echoed. "Call me every chance you get."

They arrived at a small roadside shuttle stop, where a budget-friendly airport hotel awaited. Turning off the engine, Jada bit her lip, staring at the dimly lit lot. "Guess this is it."

He exhaled, popping the door open. The weight of his duffel felt heavier than it should. "Thank you for driving me," he said quietly.

She cut the engine, stepping out to stand beside him. He noted the slight tremble in her hands as she handed him his bag. He set it down, drawing her into a tight embrace under the flickering lamppost. "It's not forever," he repeated, heart twisting at how fragile the moment felt.

Her arms wrapped around him, fingers gripping the back of his shirt. "I know," she whispered, breathing unsteadily against his chest. "Go show them how strong you are—and if it's not right, come home, okay?"

He nodded into her hair, eyes stinging. "I promise." Tipping her chin up, he kissed her—a lingering, tender exchange that tasted like longing and a muted sorrow. When they finally broke apart, she brushed tears from her cheeks, mustering a shaky smile.

"Text me from the hotel room," she said, voice wavering. "And tomorrow morning too."

He swallowed the lump in his throat. "I will."

A final, desperate squeeze of her hand, and he turned toward the small hotel entrance. She stood there, unmoving, until he disappeared through the sliding doors. Inside, he forced himself not to glance back—*Otherwise, I might never leave*, he thought.

The hotel room was unremarkable: a single bed, a flickering TV, stale air. Hakeem tossed his duffel on a chair, pulling out his phone. Immediately, he texted Jada:

In the room. Miss you already.

Her reply came seconds later:

Miss you too. Call?

He dialed, collapsing onto the bed. Her voice answered, breath uneven. "Hey," she said softly.

"Hey," he murmured, letting the tension of the day spill out. "Thank you for everything."

The hush that followed was full of unspoken fears. She cleared her throat. "Get some sleep, okay? You'll need it. I'll be waiting on the other side."

His heart clenched with a wild mix of love and regret. "I know. Sleep well, Jada."

When they hung up, the stark loneliness of the room hit him. In the silence, all he could do was replay the memory of her steady eyes, her warm arms. *I won't let this slip away again.*

Settling under the scratchy hotel sheets, he inhaled, battered by doubts and hopes. If the NFL training camp felt wrong—if his knee rebelled—he'd come back to Sweetgum with no regrets. If it felt right, he'd still have to figure out how to keep Jada in his life without fracturing them again.

Either way, he'd made a promise: no more secrets, no more leaving without a path back. He shut his eyes, mentally whispering to Jada's distant presence: *I'm doing this for me—and for us. Don't give up on me.*

Sleep crept in, restless yet determined. Tomorrow, he'd board a plane to the next chapter of his dream. But even in the midst of that dream, one clear truth resonated: *He belonged to Jada and Sweetgum first.*

CHAPTER THIRTY-FOUR

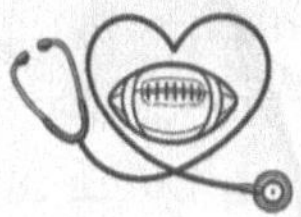

Jada paced along the sidewalk on Main Street, clutching her phone so tightly her knuckles felt numb. Afternoon sunlight spilled across the pavement, highlighting Sweetgum's quaint storefronts. A few passing neighbors greeted her, friendly smiles on their faces. She tried to return the warmth, but her heart pounded with unresolved tension. *It's day three. Why hasn't he called yet?*

She forced herself to recall the last text from Hakeem:

> Coach tossed me in new drills—super busy, sorry! Will call soon.

He'd sent that late last night. She exhaled, refusing to let worry choke her. *He's not avoiding me.* He was living in a whirlwind of workouts, medical evaluations, and playbook crash courses. *Remember, you promised to trust him.*

Still, she couldn't ignore the subtle twist in her stomach, a mixture of longing and fear. Whenever her phone buzzed, her heart jumped, but it was always just Mom checking in or the hospital staff texting about shift changes. No missed calls from him. *Calm down, Jada. He's only been gone a few days.*

Crossing the street, she spotted Rochelle and Benjamin sipping iced tea at a bench by the bookstore. Rochelle—still reigning queen of local gossip—offered Jada a sunny wave. Benjamin nodded politely.

"Hey there," Jada greeted, trying for a casual tone.

Rochelle's sharp eyes flicked to the phone in Jada's hand. "No call yet?"

Heat prickled Jada's cheeks. She wasn't surprised Rochelle guessed her exact state of mind. "Not yet," she admitted softly. "He texted, but you know… training camp is intense."

Benjamin patted Rochelle's shoulder, a wry grin on his face. "Boy's probably swamped. That league isn't all glitz. Hard work, early mornings, late nights."

Jada forced a faint smile. "I get that. I just… can't help worrying."

Rochelle's gaze softened. "You'll hear from him soon, sugar. Don't let your heart tie itself in knots. He's the one who insisted on honest communication, isn't he?"

"That's true," Jada murmured, hugging her phone closer. "Thanks."

They chatted a moment longer about the upcoming farmer's market, then parted ways. Jada made her way toward the hospital for a half-day shift, vowing not to stare at her phone every second.

LATER THAT AFTERNOON, between patient consultations, Jada ducked into her small office, scanning therapy notes for an older gentleman recovering from a knee replacement. She sat at her desk, flipping pages with mechanical focus, mind half-absent. *This is silly—he'll call when he can.*

A soft rap on the door startled her. She looked up to see

Inez, the nurse who'd become something of a friend. Inez entered with a broad smile, a stack of files in her arms.

"Hey, Dr. Davis," she said warmly. "Got some updates for your new sports PT referrals."

Jada motioned for her to set them on the desk. "Thanks, Inez."

Inez studied her face, brow quirking. "You doing okay? You seem...distracted."

Jada laughed under her breath. "Is it that obvious?"

Inez shrugged. "You're not the only one. Half the staff keeps asking if Hakeem's made the team yet." She lowered her voice, concern lacing her tone. "He call you?"

Jada's shoulders slumped. "Not yet. He texted a bit, but... it's been hectic for him."

Inez pursed her lips. "He'll call, hon. Keep your chin up."

Despite herself, Jada's tension eased a fraction. "Thanks."

As Inez departed, Jada checked her phone again. *No new notifications.* She forced a calming breath and slipped it facedown on the desk. *Focus on your patients.*

BY THE TIME she returned home, dusk had settled over Sweetgum, painting the sky in lavender hues. She flicked on a lamp, setting her bag on the couch. The apartment felt eerily silent. *No Hakeem messing with the TV, no shared dinner laughter.*

Her phone buzzed—Mom calling. Jada swallowed, already picturing the wave of questions. Still, she answered. "Hey, Mom."

"Hi, baby! Just wanted to see how you're doing," Veronica said in her usual upbeat tone. "Any news from Houston?"

Jada closed her eyes, leaning against the kitchen counter. "Not yet. He's busy with practice, I guess." She tried to sound casual, but the faint waver betrayed her anxiety.

Her mother paused, sympathy thick in her voice. "You'll hear from him soon, sweetie. He's probably exhausted. NFL training camp doesn't give them a moment's peace."

"I know," Jada admitted, a shaky exhale slipping out. "I'm just—trying not to worry. We're in a good place, but the distance is tough."

Her mom's tone gentled. "I understand. You've come so far, Jada. Give him time, trust your connection. He'll reach out when he can."

Tears pricked her eyes. "Yeah," she murmured. "Thanks, Mom."

They chatted about mundane things—family dinner plans, a cousin's upcoming baby shower—before hanging up. Jada felt marginally calmer. *I'm not alone in this. Everyone's rooting for us.*

She rummaged in the fridge, pulling out a container of left-over stir-fry. The thought of eating alone again brought a stab of loneliness. She forced herself to warm it up anyway, determined not to slip into gloom.

Halfway through her meal, her phone vibrated across the table, making her heart jump. She snatched it up—Unknown Number. *Could be him—maybe from a different phone?*

"Hello?" she said, voice tight with hope.

Static hissed, then a muffled, "Hey—" The line crackled. "—it's me. Sorry, phone died, borrowed a teammate's."

Relief and emotion flooded her. "Hakeem!" she breathed, half-laughing, half-crying. "I was worried."

"Don't be," he said, though the connection wavered. She could barely make out crowd noise in the background. "Camp's brutal. I barely get a minute to breathe. I tried calling earlier but had no signal in the dorms."

She pressed a hand to her chest, tears threatening. "I get it. Just... I'm so glad to hear your voice."

His laugh was low, tinged with fatigue. "I miss you. Everything's so fast here. My knee's holding up okay, though it's sore.

They've got me in limited contact drills for now, but it's still intense."

She swallowed. "Don't push too hard. Remember Dr. Hayes' warnings."

"I'm trying," he promised. "But coaches keep testing me. One misstep, and I'm out."

Her heart twisted. "I hate that stress for you."

"Me too," he said, voice tight. "But I asked for this, right? So... gotta see it through." Another pause, crackling static filtering in. "I probably only have a minute left on this phone. Just wanted to say... I love you, Jada. I'll call again when I can."

Tears finally slipped free, rolling down her cheeks. "Love you too," she choked. "Take care, okay?"

He exhaled, the sound of it laced with longing. "I will. Talk soon."

The line clicked, and the call ended. Jada lowered the phone, heart pounding. *At least he's okay,* she reassured herself, though the knowledge of his frantic schedule and the coaches' pressure didn't soothe her entirely.

Setting aside her half-eaten dinner, she wiped her cheeks. *We can handle this.* But as she gazed around her quiet apartment, an ache gnawed at her. They were tethered by calls and texts, mere slivers of contact in a life that felt infinitely more vibrant when he was near.

In the hush, she sank onto the couch, hugging a pillow to her chest. Eventually, exhaustion claimed her, and she let her eyes drift shut, replaying Hakeem's voice in her mind: *"I love you, Jada."* The promise of those words would have to carry her through another lonely night—until his next call reminded her that, despite the distance, they were still fighting for the same future.

CHAPTER THIRTY-FIVE

A heavy dusk pressed over Sweetgum, thick with humidity and the scent of cut grass. Jada found herself wandering Main Street after her shift, past the glow of the bakery windows and the bookstore where Rochelle was holding court with Benjamin. Couples strolled hand in hand, families spilled out of the diner with leftover pie boxes. She felt out of step with it all, a single note out of rhythm with the town's easy harmony.

Her phone was warm in her palm. The last message from Hakeem glowed on the screen: *Still in drills. Knee stiff but fine. Miss you.* Short, clipped, rushed. It had been two days since their scratchy phone call, a week since she'd seen him in person.

She tucked the phone away and pushed herself into motion, walking faster, as if she could outpace the gnaw of absence.

"Dr. Davis!"

She glanced up to see Mr. Willis waving from the rec center doorway, a stack of flyers under his arm. "We could use you Saturday for a quick injury-prevention talk with the kids."

"Of course," she called back automatically, forcing a smile. Community. Work. Distractions.

By the time she reached her apartment, her nerves still buzzed. She tried tidying the kitchen, reorganizing her bookshelves, even folding laundry. Nothing quieted the restless energy churning inside her. Finally, she carried her laptop to the balcony table, opening tabs she had no real intention of reading: medical journals, airline websites, the hospital scheduling portal. Her fingers hovered, uncertain.

If I went to Houston...

The idea had been a whisper all week, one she'd batted away as impractical. Too expensive, too risky, too much like chasing after him. But now, staring at the quiet street below, the whisper swelled into something undeniable.

Her phone buzzed. Hakim.

"Hello?" she answered quickly.

"Jada." His voice, weary but alive, poured through a crackling line. Behind him, she caught the sounds of a locker room—clanging cleats, laughter, a coach barking.

Relief loosened her chest. "You're okay?"

"Yeah. Just... drained. Camp's no joke. Knee's holding, though. I'm fighting every rep."

She closed her eyes, picturing him: sweat darkening his shirt, jaw set with determination. "I'm proud of you."

"I miss you." His voice dropped, softer now. "Feels like I only exist in borrowed minutes. I hate it."

Her throat thickened. "Me too. But you're doing what you need to."

He started to say more, but a shout in the background cut him off. "I gotta go. Curfew." His breath rushed out. "Love you."

The line clicked.

Jada lowered the phone, fingers trembling. Same pattern: brief connection, sudden silence, longing left to ache alone. She stood on the balcony until the cicadas grew loud in the twilight, the weight of distance pressing harder than ever.

Enough.

She opened her laptop again, pulse hammering, and searched flights to Houston. The numbers made her wince. She'd have to dip into her savings, rearrange her budget—but what was the alternative? Another week of pacing her apartment, second-guessing their foundation?

Her thumbs flew over the screen:

> If I came out for a weekend, would you have time?

The reply came fast, almost desperate:

> Yes. Even a few hours. Please come if you can.

That was all she needed. With a shaky breath, she selected a Friday-to-Sunday ticket, her decision cementing as the confirmation email hit her inbox.

Closing the laptop, she leaned against the balcony railing, heart racing. Fear prickled—what if the visit exposed cracks they couldn't smooth? But stronger than fear was the need to look him in the eye, to remind them both what they were fighting for.

No more pacing. No more waiting by the phone. This time, she'd bring herself to him.

CHAPTER THIRTY-SIX

The August sun was merciless, bouncing off the asphalt of the training facility's lot until it shimmered like molten glass. Hakeem swiped a hand across his forehead, pacing just inside the security gate. His phone buzzed uselessly in his palm—no new messages. Jada's plane had landed forty-five minutes ago, and still no sign of her.

He told himself it was traffic, a slow rideshare, some Houston mess she couldn't control. But every passing minute tugged tighter at his chest. He was used to waiting for things—waiting for coaches to post depth charts, waiting for trainers to test his knee—but waiting for Jada was different. Each second without her felt like wasted oxygen.

His knee ached from morning drills, the familiar pinch that told him he was skating on the edge of endurance. He shifted his weight, pretending to stretch. Teammates streamed past, tossing him quick nods or curious looks, but none of them knew what was happening in his chest. To them, he was just another long shot with an iffy knee. To him, this moment was everything.

Then a silver sedan slowed at the curb. He caught a flash of her profile through the windshield, and his breath caught. Jada.

The driver popped the trunk. She stepped out, tugging a small suitcase behind her, looking around with a guarded kind of hope. The sight of her—sunlight in her curls, her gaze searching—hit him like a punch. He waved, stepping out from the gate. Her eyes found him, widened, softened. The next thing he knew, she was crossing the sidewalk fast, suitcase wheels rattling behind her.

When she reached him, instinct overruled hesitation. He pulled her close, burying his face against her hair. Lavender shampoo, warm skin, and the faint scent of travel clung to her. He held her like a man afraid the ground might crumble.

"Jada," he breathed.

"Missed you," she whispered, her arms looping around his neck, her body trembling against his.

The tension that had coiled in him all week finally snapped loose. He let himself sink into the embrace, uncaring who saw. For the first time in weeks, he felt like himself again.

When she drew back, her eyes immediately dropped to his knee. "You're hurting."

He forced a smile. "Just sore. Morning drills were rough. Nothing I can't handle."

Her frown told him she didn't buy it, but she let it slide. Instead, her gaze swept over the looming facility behind him. "So this is it. Your new world."

"Yeah," he said quietly. "Different planet, right?"

Her eyes softened. "No. Same planet. You belong here."

He swallowed against the lump in his throat. "Come on. I've only got a couple hours before the team locks us down again. Let's make it count."

Inside, the air conditioning hit like a blast of winter. Jada's gaze darted from wall to wall—trophy cases glittering with polished brass, jerseys of legends framed under spotlights, floor tiles shining like mirrors. She slowed near a case that displayed a gleaming Super Bowl ring.

"Wow," she murmured. "This is incredible."

He rubbed the back of his neck, suddenly self-conscious. "Sometimes I look around and wonder what I'm even doing here."

Her eyes snapped to his. "Don't you dare. You've earned every inch of this, knee or no knee."

The steel in her voice both steadied and wrecked him. He guided her into a lounge tucked off the main hallway, grateful it was empty. She sank onto a couch, her suitcase at her feet, then immediately reached for his leg, palm pressing gently over the brace.

"Did you ice after drills?"

"Yes, doc," he teased, trying to lighten the weight in his chest.

She arched an eyebrow. "And?"

"And the trainers watched me like hawks."

Satisfied, she finally looked up, eyes drinking him in. "Tell me everything. Don't spare the details."

So he did. The endless drills, the suffocating pressure, the unspoken knowledge that one wrong pivot might send him home. She listened with her whole self, thumb stroking his knuckles as he spoke, her eyes never leaving his face.

"It's exhausting," she whispered.

He exhaled. "It is. But then you show up, and suddenly it feels like I can breathe again."

Her throat worked. "I couldn't just wait in Sweetgum, watching my phone like a fool. I had to see you."

Emotion swelled so fast he nearly lost words. He lifted her hand and kissed her knuckles, his lips lingering. "Thank you. I'm sorry it has to be like this—stolen hours."

"An hour with you is better than silence."

They grabbed food at the facility café—protein shakes for him, a small salad for her. They ate in a quiet corner, their hands tangled across the table. Every glance was loaded with things neither dared say too loud.

"You're staying till Sunday, right?" His voice came out low, almost reverent.

She nodded. "Hotel near the airport. I'll squeeze in calls to the hospital between, but I'm yours the rest of the time."

The words "I'm yours" hit him like gospel. He leaned forward, voice rough. "Part of me wants to forget this whole camp. Walk out with you, go home tonight."

Her eyes filled instantly. "Don't you dare. You've worked too hard."

"It's not just about football," he said fiercely. "It's about missing you so bad it hurts."

"I know." She reached across, cupping his cheek. "But if you walk now, you'll always wonder. And I won't let you carry that regret. Try, Hakeem. Even if it breaks me a little. I'll wait."

Her certainty gutted him, but also anchored him. He closed his eyes, leaning into her touch, memorizing the warmth of her palm.

Too soon, his watch buzzed. Team meeting in twenty minutes. Reality came crashing back.

He walked her to the front entrance, suitcase rolling softly behind her. Each step was a countdown he wanted to stop. At the doors, he turned, gripping her hand with both of his.

"Text me tonight," he whispered. "If I can sneak a call, I will. And tomorrow—we'll steal whatever time they let me have."

Her lips trembled, but she nodded. "I'll be waiting."

He cupped her cheek, voice breaking. "I love you, Jada."

A tear slid down her cheek. "I love you too. More than I thought possible."

Before he could think better of it, he bent and kissed her. It wasn't long—couldn't be, with staff drifting nearby—but it burned. Her breath, the salt of her tears, the desperate clutch of her hand against his chest… it felt like both a promise and a goodbye.

When he finally pulled back, she was trembling. "I'll see you tomorrow," she whispered.

He forced a nod. "Tomorrow."

She turned, tugging her suitcase through the glass doors, her figure framed by the Houston sun before vanishing from view.

For a long moment, Hakeem stood frozen, chest aching with both love and guilt. Then, with the weight of her sacrifice pressing heavy on his shoulders, he squared himself and walked back into the grind.

Every drill, every pivot, every second he lasted here—he'd make sure it was worth her faith.

It had been a week since Houston, a week since she'd stepped into Hakeem's world of locker rooms and practice fields and stolen minutes over vending machine lunches. A week since she'd clutched his hand at the airport hotel lobby, wishing their time hadn't been measured in hours instead of days.

Now, late afternoon sunlight spilled across the Sweetgum hospital corridor, long streaks of gold striping the floor as Jada made her way toward the therapy wing. The steady rhythm of work had become her lifeline—charts to read, patients to coach, stretches to guide. Predictable. Safe. But every quiet moment, the Houston weekend replayed in her head: the way he kissed her knuckles in the lounge, the way his voice cracked when he whispered he didn't want her to leave.

Her heart thumped harder. *He said roster cuts were coming in days. It's been a week. Any day now, we'll know.*

She reached her office, set her bag down, and started toward her desk when a knock interrupted her. The door pushed open and Inez peeked in, her smile gentle.

"Hey, doc. You skipped lunch again. You coming?"

Jada glanced at the clock—2 p.m. Her stomach gave a guilty twist. "Guess so. Thanks."

They walked the hallway together, their shoes clicking softly against the tile. The faint antiseptic smell mingled with the warm sweetness of cookies drifting from the volunteer bake sale stand by the elevators. Jada forced her lungs to breathe it all in, though her nerves sat like a stone in her chest.

"You hear from him today?" Inez asked, her tone careful.

Jada's shoulders sank. "No. Just a quick text last night—said camp's brutal, final decisions soon. He's too tired to talk."

Inez tipped her head, sympathy in her eyes. "Probably drowning in drills and film. Doesn't mean he isn't thinking about you."

Jada pressed her lips together. "I know. It's just the waiting. After seeing him in Houston... it's harder. I thought it'd help, but now all I do is replay those few hours in my head."

The lounge was quiet when they entered. Inez poured herself coffee; Jada dug a pre-packed salad from the fridge, appetite absent. She pushed a fork through limp lettuce leaves. *You can't live off worry, Davis.*

"He's safe, right?" Inez pressed.

"Yeah," Jada whispered. "Sore, but not injured. It's just whether the coaches believe in him." She swallowed. "And if they do, he stays in Houston. If they don't, he comes home." Her voice broke, shame prickling her skin. "Am I horrible for wanting him home, even if it means he didn't make it?"

Inez reached across the table, her hand steady on Jada's wrist. "You're human. You want both—his dream and your heart close. That's not awful. That's love being complicated."

Jada blinked fast, refusing to let the tears fall here. "Yeah," she murmured. "Complicated."

❧

Dusk clung heavy when she finally left the hospital. The evening air wrapped around her in thick humidity, pressing her scrubs against her skin. She walked to her car with her phone gripped in her palm. *Ring. Please, just ring.*

The drive home was a blur of headlights and shadows. By the time she reached her apartment, the silence inside greeted her like an unwelcome guest. She flicked on the lamp, and the yellow glow only made the emptiness starker. The couch looked wrong without Hakeem sprawled across it. The table looked wrong without takeout containers and his lopsided grin across from her. The echoes of that Houston weekend haunted every corner.

She reheated leftover soup more from discipline than hunger. As the microwave hummed, her phone buzzed. Her heart lurched. She dropped the spoon, snatching the phone. *Unknown number.*

"Hello?"

"Jada." His voice—low, ragged, achingly familiar. Relief buckled her knees.

"God, Hakeem. I was going crazy. Are you okay?"

A tired chuckle threaded through static. "As okay as camp lets me be. Coaches make final decisions tomorrow morning."

Her pulse spiked. Tomorrow. *It's tomorrow.*

"Oh," she breathed, sinking onto a stool. "Are you... how do you feel?"

"Exhausted. Knee's throbbing, but it's holding. I just wish I knew what they see when they watch me." He hesitated, his voice thick. "I miss you so much. I can't think straight sometimes."

Her eyes stung. She tried to steady her voice. "One more day. Then we'll know. If they cut you, you come home. If they keep you... we figure it out."

His breath trembled on the line. "Feels like either way I'm losing something—football or daily life with you."

Tears slipped free. "I get it. But don't hold back tomorrow. Show them everything. If you make it, we'll handle the distance. If not, we'll handle that too. Together."

He let out a broken laugh. "Where did I get so lucky?"

She covered her mouth with her hand, muffling a sob. "We're lucky. Both of us."

A muffled shout called his name in the background. He groaned. "I gotta go, babe. Meeting. I'll call the second I know tomorrow, okay?"

"I'll be waiting. I love you."

"I love you too." His whisper was fierce, like a vow, before the line went dead.

Silence fell, heavier than the humidity outside. Jada set the phone on the counter, her hands trembling as tears came unbidden. Tomorrow. The word throbbed like a drumbeat in her chest.

She tried a spoonful of soup, but it tasted flat, her throat too tight to swallow. She moved through the motions—tidying, showering, pulling on pajamas—but everything felt hollow.

When she finally crawled into bed, she clutched her phone to her chest like a talisman. Her final thoughts were prayers whispered into the dark: *Let his knee hold. Let the coaches see his heart. And let us stay strong—no matter what tomorrow brings.*

CHAPTER THIRTY-EIGHT

$\mathcal{M}$orning sunlight slanted through the tinted film-room windows, striping the carpet in gold and shadow. The air smelled faintly of stale coffee and disinfectant, though Hakeem swore he could also smell nerves—thick, metallic, sharp. Chairs scraped as players shifted restlessly, the hush punctuated by low whispers. Normally mornings began with stretching and warm-ups. Not today. Today there was no routine, no drills. Only waiting.

Final roster day.

Hakeem tapped his fingers against the side of his brace, the faint squeak betraying his tension. His shoulders were stiff, jaw tight. Across the room, two rookies murmured about rumors—who had been spotted packing, who the coaches had praised yesterday. Their words washed over him. None of it mattered. He wasn't safe until someone said he was.

If they don't see enough in me, I'm done. If they do… Houston becomes home, at least for now.

His stomach churned. He thought of Jada's voice the night before, steady despite her tears. *Show them everything you've got.*

We'll handle the rest. The memory anchored him, even as his knee gave a dull protest when he shifted.

The door creaked open. A staffer entered, clipboard in hand. The room hushed instantly, every head turning.

"Brown, Hakeem."

Hakeem's pulse kicked. He rose, legs heavy, and followed the staffer into the corridor. The hall was lined with closed office doors, each one hiding a fate being handed down. His shoes thudded against the floor, echoing louder than usual, like every step was another verdict inching closer.

At the last door, the staffer knocked, then gestured him in.

The head coach stood near a small desk, broad shoulders squared, expression unreadable. The GM sat beside him, glasses perched on the bridge of her nose, a thick file open in front of her. Their eyes lifted in unison.

"Morning," the coach said. Gruff, not unkind. "Have a seat."

Hakeem lowered himself into the chair, every nerve lit.

The coach leaned forward, forearms braced on his knees. "We've had our eye on you a while, Brown. You've got one of the strongest arms we've seen come out of a conditional invite. But—" His gaze flicked to Hakeem's brace. "That knee is still a question."

The GM's voice was cool, measured. "Medical staff sees potential, but also risk. You're not at one hundred percent."

Hakeem locked his hands together in his lap so they wouldn't tremble. "Yes, ma'am. I know. But I've been consistent in rehab. No major setbacks. I've held up in every drill they've given me."

A look passed between coach and GM. The coach exhaled slowly. "We believe you can contribute. We're offering you a spot on the practice squad to start. It's not the active roster, but if your knee proves it can handle more, we'll consider moving you up mid-season."

The words landed like a jolt of lightning. Relief. Gratitude.

The air seemed to rush back into his lungs all at once. "Yes, sir," he managed, voice raw. "Thank you."

The GM slid a stack of papers toward him. "Short-term contract. You'll travel sometimes, practice full-time, but you may not dress for games right away. Understand?"

"Yes, ma'am," he said quickly, gripping the edge of the chair. "I'm grateful for the opportunity."

The coach's gaze softened, if only by degrees. "We saw your determination. Don't waste it. The next few weeks will tell us everything."

Hakeem nodded, throat thick. "I won't. I promise."

The GM extended a hand, and he clasped it firmly. "Welcome to the Fury, Brown," she said. "Report tomorrow, six a.m. sharp. Paperwork's waiting outside."

He rose on unsteady legs, managed a respectful, "Thank you," and stepped out.

The hallway looked brighter than before. Louder, too—staff and players buzzing past—but he could barely hear them over the roar in his own chest. *Practice squad. Not cut. Not home yet... but not done either.* A grin tugged at his lips before he could stop it. He'd made it this far.

Only one person he needed to tell.

HAKEEM DUCKED into a quiet corner near the trainers' offices, the smell of antiseptic and sweat mixing faintly in the air. His brace squeaked as he knelt to dig out his phone. His hands shook as he tapped Jada's number.

It rang once. Twice.

Then her voice—sharp with anticipation. "Hakeem?"

Relief stung his eyes. "Yeah, it's me," he said softly, struggling for composure. "They're keeping me. Practice squad."

Her gasp was immediate. Then laughter, shaky and full of joy. "That's amazing! Oh my God, Hakeem, I'm so proud of you."

He pressed a hand to his forehead, fighting the wave of emotion. "Thanks. My knee's not perfect, so they're cautious. But they see enough. I've got a shot."

"That's all you needed," she whispered. Then, quieter, "So… you'll be in Houston a while?"

The grin faltered. "Yeah. At least this season. Day by day. If I prove myself, maybe longer."

The silence stretched, heavy with the weight of what it meant. Then she spoke, voice soft but steady. "I'm happy for you. Really. This is what we said—you had to try."

"Yeah." His throat tightened. "But I hate knowing it means more waiting for you. Unless… unless you'd ever think about coming here?" The words slipped out, low and tentative.

Her breath hitched. "Houston? I don't know. My job, my family… we never planned for that, not so soon."

"I know," he said quickly. "No pressure. I'd never ask you to give everything up. We can do long-distance a while. Figure it out mid-season. Just—don't think I don't want you here."

"I know you do." Her voice wavered, but there was steel under it. "And I'll visit when I can. We'll find a rhythm. I won't let distance break us."

His chest ached, but hope surged through the cracks. "I love you for that." He lowered his voice, almost whispering. "You were my first call. Soon as they told me."

A sound escaped her—half laugh, half sob. "Of course I was. I love you, Hakeem."

"I love you too."

They lingered in silence, not needing words, only the hum of connection stretching across the miles. Then duty intruded— she had patients waiting, he had paperwork and a team briefing. Neither wanted to end the call.

"Talk tonight," she whispered.

"Talk tonight," he echoed.

When the line clicked off, he stayed in the empty hallway, the weight of the phone warm in his hand. This was the dream he'd chased. And now the harder dream began: keeping the woman he loved tethered to him across distance, proving both to the coaches and to Jada that he could hold on.

Hakeem pressed a palm to his knee, feeling the steady ache beneath the brace. *Don't waste this. Don't waste her faith.*

He straightened, squared his shoulders, and stepped back into the rush of the facility. The NFL door had cracked open. Now he had to fight to stay inside—and to keep Jada's love burning strong no matter how far Houston stretched from Sweetgum.

CHAPTER THIRTY-NINE

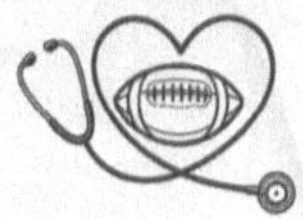

Late evening sunlight slanted through the wide lobby windows of Sweetgum Hospital, tinting the polished floor in warm streaks of orange. Jada offered a tired wave to a departing patient, her smile automatic but her mind elsewhere. The day had been a blur of therapy sessions—athletes with fresh sprains, older patients limping from joint replacements—yet she hardly felt the hours pass. Her thoughts stayed tethered to Houston.

He made it. He's actually in the NFL.

The words still felt unreal, even though she'd replayed them every night since his call. Relief had bloomed in her chest, yes—but with it came a hollow ache that didn't fade. *Am I supposed to be happy? Or scared we'll drift apart?*

She forced a polite nod at a nurse in passing and slipped down the quieter corridor toward her office. Halfway there, her phone buzzed. Her heart leapt. *Hakeem?*

But the screen showed a local number she didn't recognize. Her shoulders sagged. Probably a patient or one of the hospital lines. She nearly let it go to voicemail, but habit and restlessness had her answering.

"Dr. Davis," she said briskly, stepping aside.

"Hi, Dr. Davis, it's Alex Zhang from the rec center," came a cheerful male voice. "We ran that youth sports safety workshop together last month. Remember?"

Jada shifted her bag higher on her shoulder, recognition sparking. "Yes, of course. How are you, Alex?"

"Good, thanks. Listen, sorry for the short notice, but we're setting up another clinic—this one for basketball. We'd love to have you back, especially to talk injury prevention. Think you could spare a Saturday soon?"

The mention of Saturdays tightened her chest. Weekends were the only time she could even dream of flying to Houston. Still, the rec center needed her, and Sweetgum had always been her community. "Sure," she said carefully. "Let's pick a date. I'll see what I can juggle."

They agreed on a tentative weekend, about two weeks out. She jotted it in her phone calendar, her thumb heavy on the screen. *That's one less weekend I could see him—if I even can see him at all.*

"Thanks, Dr. Davis," Alex said warmly. "The kids really loved you last time."

After hanging up, guilt pressed down on her chest. She wanted to help here. She also wanted to be with Hakeem. She pressed her phone against her thigh, whispering, "One step at a time, Davis."

THAT EVENING, twilight smudged the Sweetgum skyline in dusky orange and violet as she unlocked her apartment. The silence that met her was the same every night—too neat, too quiet. She dropped her keys on the counter and exhaled slowly, the ache between her ribs heavy.

He'd promised to call tonight, but practice often ran late. She set her phone on the coffee table, every buzz making her pulse leap. Hours passed, the apartment filling with the drone of a TV she barely watched. By nine o'clock, frustration had her pacing. *Don't text. Don't look needy. He's busy. He'll call.*

The minutes dragged. At 10:30 she gave up, shutting off the TV. She was halfway to bed when her phone lit. Her heart shot upward.

"Hakeem?" she said breathlessly as she answered.

Crowd noise bled faintly through the line—whistles, clanging weights, voices echoing in the distance. His voice, low and tired, came next. "Hey. Sorry it's late. Just got out of meetings."

Relief buckled her knees. She collapsed onto the couch, pressing the phone close. "I was starting to worry."

"Me too," he admitted, voice rough. "Coach had us in extra film, then a roster review. Practice squad guys… we don't get to coast. Every day's a test."

Her throat tightened. "Are you okay? Knee holding up?"

"Yeah. Trainers say it's stable. Hurts, but I'm handling it. Mostly I'm running scout team—pretending to be the other team's QB in practice." He gave a dry laugh. "Not glamorous, but it keeps me sharp."

Her chest ached at the weariness in his tone. She wanted to reach through the line, press an ice pack to his knee, tell him to rest. "I'm proud of you," she whispered. "But I hate hearing how exhausted you sound."

"Part of the deal, I guess." His sigh rasped against her ear. Then, softer: "Enough about me. Tell me about your day. I want to hear something normal."

So she did. She told him about the parade of patients, about Rochelle's latest nosy comments at the café, and about Alex Zhang calling with another rec center request. He chuckled in the right places, but she could hear the fatigue pulling at him, dragging his focus away.

Eventually, he sighed. "It's almost curfew. If I don't sleep, I'll be dead at practice."

Her chest pinched. *This is all we get? Ten minutes?* But she steadied her voice. "I understand. Just… text me tomorrow. Even one word."

"I will." His voice broke. "I miss you, Jada. This isn't easy."

Her tears slipped free. "I know. We'll figure it out."

"Yeah. Goodnight." He paused, and the weight of his next words filled the silence. "Love you."

Her breath shuddered. "Love you too."

The line clicked, and the apartment's stillness swallowed her again. She pressed her forehead to her knees, sobs shaking loose. This was their life now—half-conversations and rushed check-ins, like trying to cup water in her hands.

TWO DAYS LATER, Saturday morning filled Main Street with the hum of Sweetgum life. Stalls crowded the square: crates of peaches, jars of honey, the scent of fresh bread drifting on humid air. Families strolled arm in arm, kids tugging balloons.

Jada wandered with her tote, smiling politely at greetings she barely registered. Everyone seemed to know about her quarterback boyfriend. Everyone wanted updates. She had none to give.

At a dumpling stand, Mrs. Zhang spotted her. "Jada, dear!" she called, beaming. "Come try these. New recipe."

Jada accepted the steaming sample, the rich scent curling around her.

"Any news from Hakeem?" Mrs. Zhang asked, eyes bright with mischief.

Her chest squeezed. She forced a smile. "He made the practice squad. He's working hard."

Mrs. Zhang clasped her hands together in delight. "Wonderful! But I see worry in your eyes, child."

The dumpling turned bittersweet on Jada's tongue. "It's not easy," she admitted softly. "We barely talk. I don't know if we can keep it up."

Mrs. Zhang patted her hand across the counter, her eyes kind. "When has love ever been easy? You're strong, both of you. If it's meant, you'll find a way."

Tears threatened. Jada nodded quickly, grateful for the comfort. "Thank you."

She drifted back into the crowd, Sweetgum's small-town warmth pressing in all around her. And yet, Hakeem felt farther away than ever.

THAT NIGHT, her apartment echoed with silence again. She paced with her phone in hand until nearly midnight, each passing minute carving anxiety deeper into her chest. Finally, she sent a text:

> Everything okay? Call or text when you can.
> Miss you.

No reply.

She climbed into bed, phone clutched against her pillow. Sleep came in fragments, broken by dreams of stadium lights and a phone that never rang.

At dawn, the phone was still dark. She stared at it until her eyes burned. *We can't keep going like this.*

But she forced herself up—shower, clothes, bag over her shoulder. He'd call when he could. He always would, eventually.

As she locked her door, she whispered into the stillness, "We'll figure it out. We have to."

CHAPTER FORTY

The roar of the crowd was deafening, a tidal wave of sound crashing over the turf. The stadium lights blazed like a second sun, illuminating every inch of green. Normally, the energy of a game like this would ignite him. But tonight, as he stood in full uniform for the first time since his injury, helmet tucked under his arm, Hakeem felt a knot in his chest that refused to loosen.

He scanned the stands, eyes sweeping over cheering fans, kids waving foam fingers, banners snapping in the humid air. The lower bowl shook with chants, but none of those voices belonged to Jada. He'd begged her to come, but Sweetgum Hospital couldn't spare her.

I'm here, living my dream. She's there, holding onto scraps of phone calls. The thought hollowed him out even as adrenaline coursed through his veins.

"Brown! Be ready!" an assistant coach barked.

He nodded, shoving down the ache and focusing on the game.

Late in the third quarter, the call came.

"Brown, you're in!"

Helmet strapped, heart thundering, he sprinted onto the field. The noise of the crowd surged into a roar, adrenaline igniting his muscles. This was it—his chance.

First snap—smooth. He fired a short pass, completion. Cheers rippled.

Second snap—hand-off, clean execution. The line surged forward, cleats digging, the play picking up decent yardage.

Third snap—his moment. He dropped back, eyes darting across the field. His receiver broke deep. He planted, felt the brace bite into his knee, ignored it, and launched the ball.

It sailed high, perfect arc, spiraling through the floodlights— then dropped into his receiver's hands. Thirty-yard gain. The stadium erupted.

Hakeem jogged back to the sideline, chest heaving. Coaches clapped his shoulder. Teammates slapped his helmet. For the first time in years, he felt the familiar rush of being a quarterback—being in control, delivering under pressure.

He'd done it. He'd silenced the doubt.

So why did he still feel empty?

THE FURY WON the preseason game, and the locker room turned electric. Music blared from someone's speaker, laughter echoed off the concrete walls, and reporters lurked just outside. Teammates danced, shouted, celebrated like kings.

Hakeem sat on the bench, unstrapping his pads slowly. His knee throbbed, but it had held. He'd proven himself. His phone buzzed in his bag. Jada's text lit the screen:

So proud of you. Call me when you can!

He stared at it, his throat tightening. He should be proud. He should be euphoric. But as his teammates whooped around him, all he felt was a profound clarity: the roar of the crowd couldn't compare to the warmth of her voice. The uniform couldn't fill the space she left behind.

He'd won—but not the thing he wanted most.

THE NEXT MORNING, he walked into the facility, duffel slung over his shoulder. His mind was steady.

The head coach eyed him as he stepped into the office. "Brown. You looked good last night. Best we've seen you. You're making a case for the active roster."

Hakeem swallowed hard. "Thank you, Coach. That means a lot."

The coach leaned forward. "Then why do you look like a man at a funeral?"

He exhaled, bracing himself. "Because I need to step away."

The room went still. The GM peered at him over her glasses. "Step away? You just had a breakout series."

"I know," he said quietly. "That was my dream moment. I wanted to see if I still had it. And I do. But the truth is—my heart's not here. Not really. I have someone waiting for me back home, and every second I'm here feels like I'm losing her all over again. I can't do that twice."

The coach shook his head, disbelief hardening his jaw. "You're telling me you'd walk away after proving you belong? Brown, do you know how rare that is?"

Hakeem met his eyes squarely. "I do. And that's why I can walk away with peace. I came back, I proved I could play, and I won't regret it. But I won't let this game cost me Jada. Not again."

The GM studied him, lips pressed thin. "You're sure?"

"Yes, ma'am." His voice didn't waver. "I'm sure."

The coach leaned back with a grunt. "Your call. Just know this was it. You won't get another shot."

"I don't need one," Hakeem said.

BY NOON, his forms were signed. His badge was turned in. His duffel felt strangely light as he stepped out of the facility into the hot Texas sun. The stadium loomed behind him, its steel and glass glittering. Last night it had been a dream realized. Today it was just a building he was ready to leave behind.

He inhaled deeply, chest expanding, the knot finally loosening. He wasn't walking away because he failed—he was walking away because he'd succeeded and discovered it wasn't enough.

CHAPTER FORTY-ONE

The cicadas hummed in the treeline as Jada stepped out of Sweetgum Hospital, the sliding glass doors sighing shut behind her. The heat of late afternoon clung to her skin, carrying the faint scent of honeysuckle from the edge of the parking lot. She should've felt the relief of another shift done, but her heart was heavy, a familiar ache pressing at her chest.

It had been weeks since Hakeem left for Houston. Weeks of hurried calls that ended too soon, of stolen texts squeezed between drills and film sessions. She'd told herself this was what supporting him meant—standing steady while he chased his dream. But each day without him chipped at her resolve. *I miss him more every single day.*

Fishing in her bag for her keys, she mentally mapped her evening: groceries, reheated soup, another night alone. She was so lost in the thought that at first she didn't notice the hush rippling through the staff lingering near the entrance. Laughter quieted. Eyes flicked toward the sidewalk.

"Dr. Davis!" Inez's voice rang out, bright and conspiratorial. "Looks like you've got… someone waiting for you."

Frowning, Jada turned—and the world tilted.

There he was.

Hakeem stood just beyond the hospital awning, a duffel at his feet, jeans and a plain T-shirt stretched across his broad frame. His shoulders were tense, as if braced for impact, and the sun caught on the faint outline of his brace beneath the denim. His eyes locked on hers.

"Jada," he said softly. Even through the noise of the parking lot, she heard him as if he were the only sound in the world.

Her keys slipped from her hand, clattering to the pavement. "H-Hakeem?" Her heart hammered. "What are you doing here? Did you—did you get a break from camp?"

He stepped closer, emotion thick in his gaze. "Not a break." His voice trembled but carried steady conviction. "I came back. For good."

Her breath caught, tears springing. "You… left the team?"

He nodded once, raw honesty etched across his face. "I tried, Jada. I really did. And my knee held up, but my heart didn't. Every practice, every game—I kept seeing you instead of the field. I realized the NFL dream isn't worth losing you. Not again."

Tears blurred her vision. "But—that was everything you worked for. What if you regret—"

He touched her arm gently, silencing her. "The dream changed. The truth is, what I wanted at eighteen isn't what I want now. I don't need stadium lights. I need you. I choose you, Jada. Always you."

The crowd of staff behind them faded to nothing. The whole town could've been watching, and she wouldn't have cared. She launched herself into his arms, burying her face against his neck. His arms wrapped around her with fierce relief, lifting her slightly off her feet.

Applause and whistles erupted behind them—Inez clapping, a nurse cheering, even two elderly visitors smiling knowingly.

Jada barely heard them. She inhaled his familiar scent, clung to the solid warmth of him, her tears dampening his shirt.

"I'm sorry I left you waiting," he whispered into her hair. His voice cracked. "I called the coach, packed in a day. I couldn't stand one more second away from you."

She pulled back enough to see his face, her tears spilling freely. "I'm so happy you're here," she whispered. "Happy and terrified for your knee and your future, but mostly... just happy."

He cupped her cheek, thumb brushing away a tear. "We'll figure out the rest. Coaching, training—whatever keeps me here. As long as you'll have me."

Her answer came without hesitation, voice trembling with love. "I'll have you. Forever."

His forehead pressed to hers, and then his lips found hers—soft, sure, brimming with the promise of everything they'd almost lost. The hospital staff whooped louder, but all she felt was him, here, finally, with no phone screen between them.

THEY DROVE IN HER CAR, his duffel stowed in the back. The sun dipped lower, painting the road in streaks of gold. She couldn't stop glancing sideways at him, half afraid he'd vanish if she blinked.

"So," she said at last, her voice unsteady. "You played. You proved yourself. And you still walked away."

His jaw tightened, but his hand found hers across the console. "I did. The coaches wanted me to stay, finish the season. But every day I pictured life without you—and it felt hollow. I couldn't keep pretending it was enough."

Her throat ached. "I don't want you to regret it if your knee heals stronger and you see others living that dream."

He squeezed her hand, his voice fierce. "I already proved I

could make it back. That was all I needed. But you—us—that's what makes me feel whole. Not the crowd, not the lights. You."

Her tears spilled again, quiet and hot. "Do you know how much I needed to hear that?"

"I do," he said softly. "And I swear to you—no more big decisions without you. I meant that vow, Jada. I want this life to be ours. Together."

WHEN THEY STEPPED into her apartment, it felt like a homecoming. He dropped the duffel by the couch, eyes scanning the space as if memorizing it.

"Feels like forever since I sat here with you," he murmured.

She laughed through her tears, wrapping her arms around him again. "I remember the night we promised we'd try again. Right on this couch."

His smile was tender. "And here we are. Still choosing each other."

Their lips met again, deeper this time, weeks of longing pouring out. When they finally broke apart, foreheads pressed together, she whispered, "I love you. And I'm proud of you—for proving yourself, and for knowing when to walk away."

"I love you too," he said hoarsely. "And I'm proud of us—for surviving all of it."

They sank onto the couch together, her head against his shoulder, his brace loosened as she gently massaged his knee. He hissed in relief, chuckling.

"Still my PT for life?" he teased.

"Always," she whispered.

They sat in the hush of her small apartment, wrapped in the peace of finally being whole again. Tomorrow they'd face questions, gossip, plans for the future. Tonight, they had each other.

Jada closed her eyes as he pressed a kiss to her temple. No

more distance. No more nights clutching a silent phone. He was home. And in the hum of Sweetgum's summer night, that felt like the greatest victory of all.

EPILOGUE

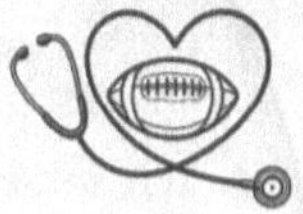

The cicadas hummed their evening chorus as Jada pushed open the chain-link gate at Sweetgum High's football field. The hinges squeaked, and she froze.

The field glowed.

Lanterns lined the turf, twinkling like a thousand fireflies, guiding her gaze to the fifty-yard line. There, waiting tall and steady beneath the fading sky, stood Hakeem. Her pulse stuttered, her throat tightening at the sight of him.

Her sandals brushed over white petals scattered across the grass—daisies. Daisies everywhere. Her chest ached with wonder. He remembered.

She reached him, breathless, and the soft glow of the lanterns turned his eyes molten with emotion.

"Remember this field?" he asked, his voice low, carrying in the hush. He gestured toward the dark scoreboard looming above. "I broke us here once. I've hated that memory ever since."

Her throat tightened. "I remember," she whispered. "It felt like the end of everything."

His hand lifted, thumb brushing her cheek, tender but certain. "I wanted to rewrite it with something better."

Her eyes caught on a small table nearby, where a simple bouquet of daisies stood beneath the lantern light. She laughed through tears. "You're definitely succeeding."

He let out a breath, steady but trembling with emotion. "Jada… I thought I needed stadium lights and roaring crowds. But every day away from you showed me the truth. My life, my joy, my future—it's here. With you. Always."

Her tears spilled over. "Hakeem—"

He dropped to one knee. The turf crunched under him, the lanterns circling like silent witnesses. From his pocket, he pulled a small velvet box and flipped it open, revealing a diamond that caught the glow of the lights and set her world spinning.

"Jada Davis," he said, voice cracking but resolute. "You gave me a second chance. You taught me what real success looks like —building a life with you. Will you marry me? Here, where I once said goodbye, I want to promise forever. No more leaving. No more regrets. Just us."

Her hands flew to her mouth, joy bursting like a tidal wave. "Yes," she cried, voice shaking. "Yes—of course, yes!"

He slid the ring onto her finger, his hands unsteady, his eyes glistening. She flung her arms around his neck, and when he rose, he kissed her—the kind of kiss that told the whole town what they had survived, and what they had chosen.

And then came the cheers.

From the bleachers, voices rose. Lanterns bobbed as people stepped forward—neighbors, friends, half the town it seemed. Rochelle and Benjamin stood hand in hand, clapping wildly. Mrs. Zhang waved a lantern high, shouting blessings in Mandarin. Inez hollered from near the gate, tears streaming as she snapped photos with her phone. Even the mayor gave a proud whistle, grinning ear to ear.

Jada froze against Hakeem's chest, startled. "You… you invited the whole town?"

He grinned, sheepish but glowing. "Sweetgum doesn't keep secrets long. And I wanted everyone to know. I wanted the world to see I'm choosing you."

Her laughter spilled out, mingling with her tears. "You're impossible."

"And yours," he murmured, pressing his forehead to hers.

The crowd surged onto the field, surrounding them in hugs, laughter, and congratulations.

Hakeem lifted her hand high, the diamond flashing under the lantern light. "She said yes!" he called, his voice carrying across the field.

The cheer that erupted shook the old bleachers, louder than any high school game had ever managed.

Jada laughed through her sobs, clinging to him as daisies swirled around their feet in the summer breeze. "I love you, Hakeem Brown," she whispered fiercely.

"I love you more, Jada Davis. Always."

As the town wrapped them in celebration, she realized this was more than an engagement. It was redemption. It was forever. The same field that once held their heartbreak now carried their triumph.

And as lantern light flickered over the scoreboard, unlit but watching, Jada knew the truth: the real victory was theirs, hand in hand, walking boldly into every tomorrow Sweetgum had waiting.

AUTHOR'S NOTE

Thank you so much for reading Play By Play, the eleventh book in the Sweetgum Meadows Romance series of stand-alone novels. I really hope you loved it! If you enjoyed this book, please consider leaving a review so that others may also find it. Also, if you haven't read the first books yet, check them out today! Although these are stand-alone novels, the stories all intertwine and progress.

I look forward to introducing you to the other characters in this lovely, family-oriented town where each couple will find their happily ever after.

Would you like to receive bonus scenes and keep up with what's next with my upcoming books? Then, make sure you sign up for my mailing list on my website by visiting ImaniPrice.com.

My full audiobook catalog is available for FREE on YouTube. Check it out here: https://swiy.co/Sweetgum

ALSO BY IMANI PRICE

Book 1: Love Between Us

Book 2: Sweet Sunsets

Book 3: Infinite Kiss

Book 4: Dance With Me

Book 5: In Charge

Book 6: Forever With You

Book 7: Secret Sweethearts

Book 8: Endless Love

Book 9: The Harder We Fall

Book 10: Reservations of the Heart

Book 11: Play by Play

Book 12: Guarded Hearts

Book 13: Healing Hearts

Book 14: Dear Sweetgum

Book 15: Lanterns of the Meadows (novella)

Book 16: Drawn to You

Book 17: Under the Sweetgum Tree

Sweetgum Meadows' Visitor's Guide

To all my lovely readers,

Thank you
for
reading